This book belongs to

The SPINDLERS

ALSO BY

Lauren Oliver

FOR YOUNGER READERS

Liesl & Po

FOR OLDER READERS

Before I Fall

Delirium

Pandemonium

Lauren Oliver

The Spindlers

ILLUSTRATED BY
IACOPO BRUNO

H
HODDER &
STOUGHTON

First published in the United States of America by
HarperCollins Childrens Books, a division of HarperCollins Publishers

First published in Great Britain in 2012 by Hodder & Stoughton
An Hachette UK company

1

Copyright © Laura Schechter 2012

Typography by Andrea Vandergrift

Illustrations by Iacopo Bruno

The right of Laura Schechter to be identified as the Author
of the Work has been asserted by her in accordance with
the Copyright, Designs and Patents Act 1988.

All characters in this publication are fictitious and any resemblance to
real persons, living or dead, is purely coincidental.

A CIP catalogue record for this title is available from the British Library.

Hardback ISBN 978 1 444 72312 0
Trade Paperback ISBN 978 1 444 72313 7

Printed and bound by Clays Ltd, St Ives plc

Hodder & Stoughton policy is to use papers that are natural, renewable
and recyclable products and made from wood grown in sustainable forests.
The logging and manufacturing processes are expected to conform to the
environmental regulations of the country of origin.

Hodder & Stoughton Ltd
338 Euston Road
London NW1 3BH

www.hodder.co.uk

To Patrick, of course—

And to my sister,
who has rescued me many times from the dark,
and for whom I would gladly go Below.

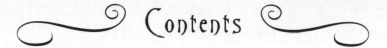

Contents

Chapter 1

THE CHANGELING, AND THE LETTERS SPELLED IN CEREAL

One night when Liza went to bed, Patrick was her chubby, stubby, candy-grubbing and pancake-loving younger brother, who irritated and amused her both, and the next morning, when she woke up, he was not.

She could not describe the difference. He looked the same, and was wearing the same pair of ratty space-alien pajamas, with the same fat toe sticking out of the hole in the left foot of his red socks, and he came down the stairs exactly the same way the real

Patrick would have done: *bump*, *bump*, *bump*, sliding on his rump.

But he was not the same.

In fact, he was quite, quite different.

It was something in the way he looked at her: It was as though someone had reached behind his eyes and wrung away all the sparkle. He walked quietly—too quietly—to the table, sat nicely in his chair, and placed a napkin on his lap.

The real Patrick never used a napkin.

Nobody else noticed a thing. Mrs. Elston, Liza's mother, continued sorting through the stack of bills on the kitchen table, making occasional noises of unhappiness. Liza's father continued passing in and out of the room, his tie unknotted and wearing only one sock, muttering distractedly to himself.

The fake-Patrick picked up his spoon and gave Liza a look that chilled her to her very center.

Then the fake-Patrick began to eat his cereal, methodically, slowly, fishing all the alphabet letters out of his Alpha-Bits one by one and lining them up along the rim of his bowl.

Liza's heart sank. She knew, at that moment, what had happened, as well as she knew that the sky was up and the ground was down and if you turned around fast enough in a circle and then stood still, the world would keep turning the circle for you.

Patrick's soul had been taken by the spindlers. And they had left this thing, this not-younger-brother, in its place.

"Mom," she said, and then, when her mother did not immediately respond, tried again a little louder. "Mom."

"Mmm?" Mrs. Elston jumped. She squinted at Liza for a moment, the same way she had looked at the instruction sheet that came along with the Easy-Assemble Coffee Table in Mahogany, the one she had had to return to the store after she could not figure out how to screw the legs on.

"Patrick's being weird," Liza said.

Mrs. Elston stared blankly at her daughter. Then she whirled around, suddenly, to her husband. "Did you ever pay the electric bill?"

Mr. Elston didn't seem to hear her. "Have you seen my glasses?" he asked, lifting the fruit bowl and peering underneath it.

"They're on your head."

"Not *those* glasses. My reading glasses."

Mrs. Elston sighed. "It says this is our final notice. I don't remember a first notice. Didn't we pay the electric bill? I could have sworn . . ."

"I can't go to work without my glasses!" Mr.

Elston opened the refrigerator, stared at its contents, closed the refrigerator, and rushed out of the room.

Across the table, the fake-Patrick began rearranging the cereal letters on the outside of his bowl. He spelled out three words: I H-A-T-E Y-O-U. Then he folded his hands and stared at her with that strangely vacant look, as though the black part of his eyes had eaten up all the color.

Liza's insides shivered again. She slid off her chair and went over to her mother. She tugged at the sleeve of her mother's nightgown, which had a small coffee stain at its elbow. "Mommy."

"Yes, princess?" she asked distractedly.

"Patrick's freaking me out."

"Patrick," Mrs. Elston said, without looking up from her notepad, on which she was now scribbling various figures. "Stop bothering your sister."

Here's what the real Patrick would have done: He would have stuck out his tongue, or thrown his napkin at Liza in retaliation, or he would have said, "It's her *face* that's the bother."

But this impostor did none of those things. The impostor just stared quietly at Liza and smiled. His teeth looked very white.

"Mom—" Liza insisted, and her mother sighed

and threw down her pencil with so much force that it bounced.

"*Please*, Liza," she said, with barely concealed impatience. "Can't you see that I'm busy? Why don't you go outside and play for a bit?"

Liza knew better than to argue with her mother when she was in a mood. So she went outside. It was a hot and hazy morning—far too hot for late April. She was hoping to see one of the neighbors out doing something—watering a plant, walking a dog—but it was very still. Liza almost never saw the neighbors. It was not that kind of neighborhood. She didn't even know most of their names: only Mrs. Costenblatt, who was so old she looked exactly like a prune.

Today, as on most days, Mrs. Costenblatt was sitting on her porch, rocking, and fanning herself with one of the Chinese delivery menus that were often stuck—mysteriously, invisibly, in the middle of the night—under the front door.

"Hello," she called out to Liza, and waved.

"Hello," Liza called back. She liked Mrs. Costenblatt, even though Mrs. Costenblatt hardly ever moved except to rock in her chair, and could not be counted on to do anything interesting.

"Would you like a glass of lemonade?" Mrs. Costenblatt called out. "Or a cookie?" She offered

Liza lemonade and a cookie every time they saw each other, unless it was winter, in which case she offered hot chocolate and a cookie. Mrs. Costenblatt liked to rock even in cold weather, and she would appear on her porch so bundled in blankets and scarves, she looked like an overstuffed coatrack.

"Not today, thank you," Liza said regretfully, as she always did. She was not allowed to accept things to eat or drink from Non-Family Members. Liza often wished the rule applied to Family Members instead. She would much rather have had one of Mrs. Costenblatt's cookies than her aunt Virginia's tuna casserole.

She wondered whether she should tell Mrs. Costenblatt about Patrick, but decided against it. Two weeks earlier, at recess, when she had tried to tell Christina Millicent and Emma Wong about the spindlers and the constant threat they posed, they had laughed at her and called her a liar. Mrs. Costenblatt was a good listener—partly, Liza thought, because she couldn't hear very well—but Liza didn't want to risk it.

There was only one thing that Liza hated more than liars, and that was being accused of being one.

At one edge of the yard, a pile of pinecones had

been neatly stacked. Liza had arranged them this way only yesterday, thinking that she and Patrick might play a round of Pinecone Bowling in the morning. But of course she could not play with the false Patrick; he would no doubt find a way to cheat.

She had a sudden, wrenching, fierce desire for Anna, her old babysitter, to come home. She would have played Pinecone Bowling. In fact, she had invented it.

Last fall Anna had gone away to college, which meant that she had moved and couldn't babysit anymore, and instead Liza and Patrick were left with Mandy, who always chewed her gum too loudly and didn't like to play games—she didn't like anything, really, except talking on the phone. Anna had come over to babysit several times during her Christmas vacation, but on her spring break she had gone away with her friends. Liza and Patrick had gotten a water-warped postcard from her, but most of the writing had been too blurry to read.

In addition to the postcard she had sent from the beach, she had sent two letters from college, and a white sweatshirt with a fierce-looking bear on the front, explaining in the attached note that it was her school's mascot. Patrick had cried like a baby when it turned out the sweatshirt was in Liza's size, and she had finally lent it to him. He had promptly spilled tomato sauce on it, and she'd refused to speak to him for an entire day.

Liza knew it was stupid, but sometimes she fantasized that Anna would turn up again and confess her deepest secret: that Liza and Patrick were, in fact, her siblings, and they had all been torn apart by some horrible event when they were little and forced into different families.

Liza's fantasies were a little hazy after that point, but she thought that somehow she, Anna, and Patrick would end up on a long journey together, hunting down some of the magical creatures Anna had always told them about, like gnomes and nimphids (who were beautiful but bad-tempered).

Liza sighed. Anna would also have known what to do about the spindlers. She was, after all, the person who had first told Liza and Patrick about them. She was the one who had warned them about the strange spider creatures and had told them what they must do to be protected.

Liza scanned the yard for gnomes, but saw nothing. Only last week, Patrick—the real Patrick—had spotted one scampering into the rhododendron.

"Look, Liza!" he had cried out, and she had turned just in time to see a hard, brown hide, which was as cracked and weathered as a leather purse.

It was too hot for the gnomes today, Liza decided. Anna had told Liza they preferred cool climates.

Liza pressed her face up against the small fir tree that stood next to the birdbath, inhaling deeply. It was easier to see the magic through its branches, she found. The scratchy needles poked deeply into her skin, and she stood and squinted through the layers of green. Looking at the world through the fir tree meant seeing only the essential things: the vivid green of the grass, dew glistening on petals, a robin flicking its tail, a squirrel rustling through the rhododendron, a miracle of life and growth that forever pulsed under the ordinariness.

And, of course, it was only when looking through the tree that you could make a wish and have it come true—Anna had also told them that.

Liza spoke a wish quietly into the scratchy branches.

We will not repeat it. Everyone knows that only wishes that are kept secret will ever come true. But know this: The wish was about Patrick.

Liza heard a step behind her. She turned and saw the Patrick-who-was-not-Patrick standing on the

9

front porch, watching her.

Liza sucked in a deep breath, gathered her courage, and said, "You are not my brother."

Not-Patrick stared at her with flat blue eyes. "Yes, I am," he said calmly.

"You aren't."

"Am too."

"Prove it," Liza said, crossing her arms, and she tried to think of a question whose answer only the real Patrick would know. She was quiet for a bit. At last she asked, "When you are playing hide-and-seek on a rainy day, what is the best hiding space?"

"Behind the bookcase in the basement," not-Patrick answered automatically. "In the crawl space that smells like mold."

Liza was disappointed. He had gotten it right; this fake-Patrick was obviously smarter than she gave him credit for—smarter, she wouldn't wonder, than the real Patrick. (Though that wasn't saying much. Only a week ago the real Patrick had tried to turn the basement into a swimming pool by flooding the sink! Absurd.) Maybe she needed to ask a harder question.

"What must you do every night before you go to sleep?" Liza said, eyeing the not-Patrick narrowly to see whether there was any hesitation or shiftiness in his answer.

But he responded promptly, drawing a big X across his chest, "You must cross yourself once from shoulder to hip and say out loud, 'Sweep, sweep, bring me sleep. Clear the webs from my room with the bristliest broom.'"

Liza was stunned. She had been sure—positive!—that the question would baffle not-Patrick, but his answer was correct, and he stood looking at her with an expression of triumph. When Anna had first discovered the spindlers, she had invented this rhyme as a way of keeping the spindlers at bay while they slept. Everyone knows there is nothing a spider fears more than a broom, and someone sweeping with it, and the broom charm had, in fact, protected them for years.

Patrick—the real Patrick—must have forgotten to say the broom charm last night before he went to sleep. He and Liza had been fighting—Patrick had accused her of stealing his favorite socks, which were blue and embroidered with turtles, as though she would ever have worn anything so ridiculous—and Liza called him paranoid, and when he did not know what that meant, he stormed into his room and slammed the door.

He was distracted; that must be why he had not said the broom charm. Liza felt a heavy rush of guilt. It was her fault, at least partially.

And so the spindlers had gotten him: They had dropped down from the ceiling on their glistening webs of shadowed darkness and dropped their silken threads in his ear, and extracted his soul slowly, like a fisherman coaxing a trout from the water on a taut nylon fishing line. In its place they deposited their eggs; then they withdrew to their shadowed, dark corners and their underground lairs with his soul bound closely in silver thread.

And the soulless shell would wake the next morning, and walk, and talk, as not-Patrick was walking and talking.

But eventually, the soulless shell would crumble to dust, and a thousand spindlers—nested and grown—would burst forth, like a lizard hatching from an egg. And distraught parents would wake up, believing their children to have been kidnapped while they slept, and they would appear tearfully on television, begging for their children's safe return, when really the spindlers were to blame.

Liza felt a sudden tightness in her throat.

"You see!" not-Patrick crowed. "I told you. I *am* your brother."

Then Liza was struck by an idea.

"Come here," she said to not-Patrick, and even though she was filled with revulsion by the closeness

12

of this imitation, this cold and cardboard thing, she forced herself to stand still as he approached.

Suddenly she lunged for him and began tickling his stomach.

The real Patrick was extraordinarily ticklish and would have screamed with laughter and tried to shove Liza off and begged for mercy. Liza loved the sound of Patrick's laugh. It came in short, explosive bursts, as though each time he was relearning how to do it.

This Patrick stood still, watching her dully. "What are you doing?" he asked.

Liza pulled away. She then had the same feeling she'd had several years ago, when she had swung too high and too fast on the swings at the playground, and the world teetered underneath her: a feeling of triumph but also of terror. She knew it. This Patrick was not the real Patrick. And that meant that the soul of the real Patrick had been bound up in silver thread and carried deep underground, and that inside the body of not-Patrick, insects were nesting.

Liza drew herself up to her full four feet four inches. "I am not afraid of you," she said to not-Patrick, but she was of course speaking to all those infant spindlers sleeping soundly in their thousands of soft eggs, somewhere deep inside his chest. And of course she *was* afraid. She was more afraid than she had ever been in her life. "I will find my real brother, and I will bring him back."

And then she spun quickly on her heel and stalked off toward the house, so not-Patrick and the tiny monsters he carried inside him would not see that she was shaking.

Chapter 2

Mrs. Elston

SEVERAL FALSEHOODS
AND ONE BROOMSTICK

All afternoon Liza tried to remember what Anna
had told her about spindlers. She thought
about asking her mother whether she still had Anna's
cell phone number, but at the last minute decided
against it. What if Anna was busy doing something
Important and got angry when Liza called? Worse,
what if she didn't remember Liza at all?

Instead she got out a notebook and made a little
list for herself: "Everything I Know About Spindlers
and Their Habits."

Spindlers were not like regular spiders. They had eight legs, of course, but at the end of their legs they had human hands; and they had only two eyes, like a person's, although their eyes were enormous and crescent-shaped, and they could see perfectly well in even the darkest night. Furthermore, though they were often as small as a pinhead, they could quite easily swell to the size of a house cat or larger. Some of the largest spindlers could grow to the size of a car, and in their large-jawed mouths they had one hundred teeth, each as sharp as a fang.

She did not know what the spindlers did with the souls that they stole. Anna had claimed that she did not know either, although Liza had never quite believed her; Anna had always gone white when Liza mentioned them, as though someone had just punctured her chin and drained all the color from her face.

She did know that spindlers were practically indestructible. Even brooms would not kill them.

She did not know how to kill a spindler, or whether it was even possible.

And that frightened her.

That night, she washed her face and put on her pajamas and brushed her teeth—standing as far as

possible from not-Patrick, who brushed his teeth duti-
fully beside her (another thing the real Patrick, who
despised brushing his teeth and used as many tricks
as possible to get out of it, would not have done).

Both of them were now pretending that everything was back to normal. It was a game they had
entered into by silent agreement. Liza pretended not
to know that Patrick was not really Patrick; and
Patrick pretended both that he was himself and that
Liza believed that he was himself. It was a difficult
game, but fortunately Liza was used to playing games
with her brother.

"Will you tell me a story?" the not-Patrick asked,
as the real Patrick might have after they had both
rinsed and placed their toothbrushes side by side in
the toothbrush stand. Liza was careful to swivel her
bristles away from his so they would not be touching.

"Not tonight," Liza said, struggling to keep her
voice normal and cheerful. Liza often snuck into the
real Patrick's room and told him stories late into the
night.

"Why not?" He stared at her with large, hollow
eyes.

Liza knew what he was doing. He was trying to
lure her into his bedroom, where the spindlers would
be waiting—hundreds of them—to steal her soul as

soon as she closed her eyes.

"I'm too tired tonight," she said. "Maybe tomorrow night."

Not-Patrick shrugged. "Fine," he said, his eyes flashing angrily. "I didn't want to hear one of your stories anyway." Liza thought about the letters lined up on the rim of his bowl this morning: I H-A-T-E Y-O-U. She thought, too, of their argument last night, and how it was her fault that Patrick had forgotten to say the broom charm.

And yet only yesterday Patrick had run up to her, laughing, cupping a tiny rose-colored newt in his muddy palms, and asked her whether they could keep it together, as a pet. And in that second her hatred for the spindlers was so intense she had to grip tightly to the porcelain sink.

She waited until he had gone into his bedroom and closed the door. Then she shoved her feet into a pair of her favorite sneakers without bothering to put on socks, and padded carefully down the broad, carpeted stairs into the living room. For a moment she paused, listening to her parents' muffled voices; they were in the den.

"It'll be all right," her father was saying.

Her mother responded, "And now you'll need new glasses. And Liza will need braces in the fall. And we never fixed that leak in the basement. . . ."

Liza continued through the kitchen and to the small pantry, where her parents kept rolls and rolls of paper towels, bottles of ketchup, and cleaning supplies. She found the broom and returned down the hallway. She needed a Plan, and she was so busy thinking of one she forgot to dodge the creaky floorboard just next to the hall table.

She knew at once she had been too loud. Her parents went silent, and a moment later the door to the den swung open, and a triangle of blue light appeared in the hallway.

"Liza?" her mother called to her. "Is that you?"

Liza came forward obediently, clutching the broom.

"What on earth are you doing?" Mrs. Elston said. "Why aren't you in bed?" She was standing in the doorway of the den, and there was a small, dark crease between her eyebrows, like a tiny exclamation point. There was often an exclamation point between her eyebrows, and Liza liked to imagine invisible words written before it: *Liza, please! Just give me a second! You're driving me crazy!* All these words were implied by that little black crease.

Behind her, Liza's father was holding his book at arm's length, since he had not found his reading glasses, despite his insistence that they could not just get up and walk on their own.

Liza took a deep breath. She had been told repeatedly by her parents that it was wrong to lie, so she said, "I am going to find Patrick."

"Patrick? What do you mean? Isn't he in bed?"

Liza explained, "The pretend-Patrick is in bed. I'm going to find the real Patrick."

Mrs. Elston rubbed her eyes. "Please, Liza. I'm begging you. Don't start this now. It's past your bedtime. Put the broom where you found it and go to your room."

"I need the broom," Liza insisted. She did not like to be so much trouble to her mother, but it would be insanely impractical to try to launch a sneak attack on a mass of spindlers without at least a broom handy to frighten them off, and Liza was both very sane and extremely practical. "Spindlers are afraid of brooms. They'll leave me alone if they see I'm carrying one. At least, I hope they will." A shiver of fear zipped up her spine, and she clutched tightly to the broom handle.

"Spinners?" Mrs. Elston repeated, and the exclamation point danced up and down. "What on earth are you talking about?"

"Not spinners. Spind-lers." Liza said the word slowly, so her mother would be sure to understand. "Spider people who live underground. They're the ones who've got Patrick."

For a moment Mrs. Elston did not say anything. She drew her mouth into a thin white line, and this reminded Liza of many things, none of them pleasant: of ruled notepaper, on which she was expected to write boring things at school; of rulers and long marches through endless hallways, and walls everywhere she looked.

Then Mrs. Elston's face seemed to collapse, like a balloon deflating. She said in a tired voice, "Liza. We've talked about your stories before, haven't we?"

Liza was not fooled by the quietness. She shifted her weight from foot to foot. "Y-yes."

"And what have we said?" The tiredness was even worse, Liza thought, than anger. The tiredness seemed to say, *I have nearly had enough of you.*

"We said that I'm not supposed to," Liza said.

"Not supposed to what?" Mrs. Elston prompted her.

"Not supposed to make up stories," Liza said, and swallowed. She was gripped in an agony of humiliation. It felt like a giant fist was squeezing her from all sides. She wished fervently that Anna would come back right then, in that second; she would push open the door, her long blond braid swinging down her back. Anna knew; Anna understood. She and

Patrick were the *only* two people Liza had ever met who knew, who really believed, that the real world was not just grocery stores and park playgrounds, textbooks and toilet paper. They knew that it was gnomes, and spindlers, and different worlds, too.

"And why is that?" Mrs. Elston said.

Liza swallowed hard. "Because I'm too old." She gripped the broom handle. She shifted from right to left. She imagined she was skating.

"Exactly," Mrs. Elston said. "Go put away the broom, tuck yourself into bed, and go to sleep, like a good girl." She turned to Mr. Elston. "Robert? A little help?"

Mr. Elston finally looked up from his book. He squinted at Liza from across the room. "Listen to your mother, Liza," he said, and returned to his book.

It was too much. That was the problem with grown-ups; they told you not to lie, and then got angry when you told the truth!

It was *not fair.* Liza burst out, "But I'm not making it up! The spindlers really did take Patrick. That thing in his bed—it's not really him. It only looks like him. I told you so this morning, and you didn't listen, and I knew you wouldn't listen, because you never listen, which is why I'm going looking for him myself."

Liza shut her mouth quickly, feeling breathless. She knew at once she had gone too far. She never raised her voice to her mother—ever.

The color drained from Mrs. Elston's face, as though someone had just filled her to the brim with milk. "You're very bad to speak to me that way, Liza," she said sadly.

Liza felt a flare of guilt, and tried to squash it by feeling angry again. But she couldn't. She could only feel guilty, and then sorry for herself, and sorry for her mother, and sorry that she had made her mother sorry, and then guilty again.

"Now go to your room," Mrs. Elston said quietly. "We'll talk about this in the morning."

Liza squeezed the broom handle, turned, and ran up the stairs.

At the top of the stairs she paused. Her heart was drumming in her chest, and it seemed to echo the words still running endlessly through her mind: *notfair notfair notfair.*

The only light came from a small, single nightlight, which burned just outside the bathroom and cast a faint red circular glow on the carpet.

She could turn left and go down the hall to her own bedroom, and curl up safely in bed with the broom next to her footboard, and sleep safely and soundly, as her mother surely would have wanted her to do.

Or she could turn right and go down the hallway in the other direction to her brother's room, and she could keep watch over the monster, and see if she could find out what had happened to the real Patrick.

"I am not afraid," Liza said quietly to herself, and forced her body to turn to the right. "I am not afraid," she repeated, and took one step, and then another. She was alarmed by how quickly she came to Patrick's door, with its smudgy door handle and various scrawled pictures of alien ships and underwater animals taped across it.

I can still go back, thought Liza. *I can look for the real Patrick tomorrow.*

But she knew that tomorrow might be too late.

Instead she reached out and grabbed the doorknob; then she eased open the door and slipped into the blackness of her brother's room.

It was perfectly quiet except for the heavy pounding of Liza's heart. The normal Patrick would have been snoring loudly, and snuffling, and rustling about in his bed; Liza could hardly stand to share a bed with him when they went on vacations. He would kick and toss all evening.

But the not-Patrick slept soundlessly and in perfect

stillness, like a stone. Liza reminded herself that he might as well have been a stone. Soon he would break apart completely, and then there would no hope for his rescue.

The warm, glowing center of him—the live thing—was no doubt buried somewhere deep underground by now.

Liza knew she had no choice. She, too, must go Below.

Chapter 3

Mr. Elston

THE BASEMENT

During the day, Liza liked the basement. She and Patrick often played hide-and-seek among the large boxes, which were full of old sweaters and yellowing books and broken toys and other interesting things. When it rained, there was a leak in the corner, just above the old, yellowing map, which was warped and bubbled from moisture, and which depicted cities and countries that had long ago ceased to exist; then Mr. Elston would have to come, stomping and cursing, to set up a bucket between the boxes.

But in the night it was very different.

Liza had waited until both of her parents had gone to bed; then she had slipped on a long-sleeved shirt and her favorite puffy vest over her pajamas, and made her way as quietly as possible to the door next to the kitchen, and then down the rough wooden stairs that led into the basement. Everything looked strange and sharp and unfamiliar. The piles and boxes were people wearing cloaks of darkness; any of them might jump out and grab her at any second. Liza was desperately tempted to turn on the light. But then, of course, the spindlers would know she was coming. Liza thought she heard something rustle behind her, and she spun around, clutching the broom with both hands like a baseball bat.

But no. There was nothing. Liza lowered the broom.

There it was again. Liza paused, listening. Faintly, she could detect the sounds of scratching and scrabbling, coming from her right. She took one shuffling step in that direction, and then another. Despite the hours and hours she had spent playing in the basement, she felt very turned around: She had the sense that the room was growing bigger all around her, extending outward in strange and twisty ways, like a tightly closed flower suddenly opening its petals.

She bumped her knee against a hard corner and

said, "Crill," quietly into the dark. *Crill* was her word for when things were going badly.

She reached out and moved her hand along the object blocking her path; she recognized the carvings along its surface as belonging to a large wooden trunk in which her mother kept woolen sweaters. This helped orient her, and Liza took several more steps forward, more confidently this time. She kept the broom in front of her and swept from side to side so she could be sure that the path was clear and she would not trip and fall over anything.

She thought if she were to break her neck and die, and then Patrick—the fake one—were to crumble to dust when the spindlers overtook him, their parents would be extremely sorry and regret that they had accused Liza of making up stories. The idea was somewhat pleasing, and helped her focus on something other than the fear, and the scratching sounds of so many tiny nails, which were growing louder by the second.

At last she stood in front of the narrow bookcase that concealed the hole in the wall that was a crawl space: the best place for hiding during games of hide-and-seek. Behind the bookcase, the sounds of scratching and clicking were louder than ever.

Liza thought of her warm bed upstairs, and the

orderliness of her room, with her pink-and-white-striped chair and the dollhouse she never played with anymore but still enjoyed looking at, pretty and peak-roofed and painted white. Inside the dollhouse were figures of a father and a mother and a brother and a sister with smiles painted on their faces, sitting happily around a miniature dining room table topped with a bowl of miniature fake fruit.

There was no basement in the dollhouse. There were no spindlers there, either.

But the dollhouse was not real life, and Liza knew that. As we have already established, she was a very practical girl.

She turned and gave a final glance behind her. The basement appeared vast and black, as though it had been consumed by a fog: She could make out nothing but the very barest outlines of dark shapes in the mist.

She turned back toward the bookcase. She placed the broom carefully on the ground by her feet. Then, using both hands, she shoved and wiggled and inched the bookcase along the wooden floor, until slowly the hole in the wall was revealed.

This, too, appeared to have grown larger. Normally Liza had to double forward and squeeze herself into the crawl space when she wanted to hide, and even then she had to be careful not to move around too much or she would bang her elbows on the walls or her head on the ceiling.

But now she stood at the edge of an enormous, gaping circle, twice as tall as she was. She could see nothing but a few feet of rough dirt pathway; beyond that, everything was blackness. She heard a howling wind that seemed to be blowing from somewhere miles and miles away. It carried with it strange smells that reminded Liza of very old paper, and the mud that clogged the storm drains in the spring.

She bent down, retrieved her broom, and walked forward into the hole. The ground beneath her feet was crisscrossed with faint silvery threads, all pulsing faintly in the dark, as if illuminated by a strange, evil energy. There could be no doubt that the spindlers had been here. This must be how they came in and out, up and down.

Liza took only a few steps before the darkness swallowed her completely. The air was cold and damp and weighed on her like a terrible, sweaty hand. The smell of mud and decay grew stronger and fouler as the ground sloped steeply downward.

She went slowly, gropingly forward, terrified that at any second she would trip and fall and be sent into a wild hurtle into black space. She had the sense of walls pressing down on her, but when she swept from side to side with her broom, she encountered no resistance: nothing but air.

Then, from her left, she heard the unmistakable sounds of scratching: louder, much louder than she had thought possible.

Bigger.

Liza froze. Fear drove through her, an iciness in her veins. She gripped the broom so tightly in her hands, her knuckles began to ache.

No. Now the scratching was on her right.

Closer. Closer.

Behind her.

Just like that, the terror that was ice in her veins became a gushing tidal wave, and Liza began to run. She ran blindly through the dark, her heart scrabbling into her throat, suppressing a cry of terror, stumbling over uneven ground. From all around her—above and behind, on her left and her right—came the sound of scratching feet and claws.

Then her foot snagged on something hard, and Liza tripped, and just as she had feared, went hurtling downward into the dark.

Chapter 4

Liza

THE RAT

First there was rushing wind; and then a warm, dark fog; and then a tremendous snapping and crackling sound as Liza passed through what seemed like a floating pile of dried autumn leaves.

"Oof." After several seconds, she landed on her back on a large fur rug. Dizzy and disoriented, she sat up, relieved to find that the broom had fallen just a few feet away from her and appeared undamaged.

Above her, dark branches covered with glossy purple leaves and strung with hundreds and hundreds of lanterns formed a kind of vaulted ceiling. In one place, the leaves and branches had been broken apart where she had passed through them, and a Liza-size shape was now imprinted in the ceiling. Pretty, lace-edged leaves, disrupted by her fall, swirled through the air around her.

"Excuse me," came a muffled voice from directly underneath her. "But this position is really quite uncomfortable. Quite squashily uncomfortable."

Liza yelped, and scrambled to her feet.

The fur rug shook itself, unfolded, and stood.

Liza gaped. She saw that it was not a fur rug at all.

It was a rat.

It was the largest—and also the strangest—rat Liza had ever seen. Rather than scuttling around on all fours, first of all, it was standing on its hind legs, and it was so tall it reached almost nose to nose with Liza. It was, second of all—Liza blinked, and rubbed her eyes, and couldn't believe it—wearing *makeup*. A thick band of red lipstick circled her narrow lips—Liza assumed the rat was a female, given her appearance—and clots of mascara darkened the tufts of fur above her sparkling black eyes.

Perched on her head was what Liza could only imagine must be a wig of the rat's own creation: It was made of bits and pieces of different materials, wire and thread and yarn and even some pale yellow hair Liza thought she recognized from the head of her old doll, Amelia. The wig was perched at a slightly rakish angle on the rat's head, like a hat; two braids framed the rat's narrow face.

The rat was also wearing *clothes*. She wore a shawl of lace wrapped around her shoulders and belted at her waist with a bit of knotted rope. And she wore a skirt that appeared to have been glued together with bits and pieces of newspaper. The rat was not, however, wearing any shoes, and Liza saw her strange black feet and long black claws. Rather than letting her tail drag on the ground, the rat carried it slung over one arm, almost like a purse.

Liza did not especially like rats. (Does anybody like rats?) But she thought this must be the most awful-looking rat she had ever seen in her whole life.

The rat had bent down to scoop up a small paper hat, like the kind Liza used to wear as a little kid at birthday parties, which had been flattened.

"You ruined it," the rat said reproachfully as she tried, and failed, to return the hat to its proper shape. "Who taught you to go around falling on rats and squishing on hats? Terrible, terrible. Must always be mindful of your manners."

"I didn't mean to," Liza said. "I tripped."

The rat sniffed. "Likely story." She placed the now-deformed hat on top of her hideous wig, making the animal look even more bizarre than before. Liza unconsciously took a step backward.

"Now, now, no reason to be scuttling away from me," the rat said. "I'm not going to eat you."

This was not very comforting to Liza, as she had not been considering the possibility of being eaten until the rat tried to reassure her. But then she did consider it, and felt extremely queasy.

Still, she said, "I'm not afraid," and tried to keep her voice steady.

"You're not?" The rat looked pleased. "Oh, how wonderful. How very, very wonderful. I really do hate it—everyone always shrieking and running— and reaching for brooms—brooms!" She stopped and peered at Liza. "You're not planning to poke me with your broom, are you?"

Liza was unprepared for the question. "N-no," she stuttered out.

"Or bop me over the head?"

"Of course not," Liza said.

"Or stick its handle in my eye? Or try to tickle my nose with its bristles?"

"No, no, no." She began to feel offended. "I would never."

The rat appeared satisfied. "Then you may have it back, I suppose." With a surprisingly graceful movement, she bent forward at the waist, snatched the broom from the ground, and handed it back to Liza with the arm—or paw, or whatever it was—around which her tail was looped.

"Now let's have a good look at you." Once again, the rat doubled forward and snatched up a plastic lunch box, which she must have been carrying before Liza went tumbling into her. The rat fished around inside it for a moment before extracting a pair of glasses, which she then placed ceremoniously on her nose. The lenses made the rat's eyes appear golf ball–size.

Liza let out an excited shout. "Where did you get those?" she asked. She knew those wire-frame glasses, with the masking tape that kept the bridge intact.

The rat immediately whipped them from her nose. "I've always had them," she said.

"You haven't," Liza said. She reached out and wrenched them from the rat's paw. "Those are my father's reading glasses."

"I tell you, they're mine!" the rat said shrilly.

But Liza had just caught a glimpse of another familiar item inside the rat's lunch box, and she grabbed it and squatted down to rifle through it.

"These are Patrick's socks!" she cried out, extracting the socks that had been the source of all her trouble: the blue ones, embroidered with turtles. "And my missing math homework! And Patrick's baseball!" She wrapped her father's glasses in the socks and tucked the bundle carefully into the right pocket of the vest she was wearing over her long-sleeved shirt. The baseball went in the left pocket of her pajama pants; she heard a small rip in the fabric as she wedged it down and against her leg. The homework she left in the lunch box. She doubted very much that Mr. Toddle would accept as an excuse that a rat had stolen it. She didn't recognize the other things—several more socks, a rusted key, a saltshaker, and a purple hair scrunchie—but she bet that they, too, had been taken from the world above. "You stole them."

The rat bent down and jerked the lunch box away from Liza. She snapped and latched it closed, and then straightened up again. Liza stood as well, so the rat would not tower over her.

"I did no such thing!" the rat replied in a tone of deep indignation. "I bought them fair and square from the troglods."

"The *what*?" Liza said.

"The troglods." The rat paused and peered at Liza. "Don't tell me you've never heard of the troglod market."

Liza shook her head.

"My dear child!" the rat exclaimed. "Where *have* you been? It's just around the corner. It's late, but with any luck we might still snatch a sight or two. Come along. Follow me."

The rat was already bustling off.

"No!" Liza burst out, more loudly than she intended. The rat stopped and looked at her quizzically. "I—I don't have time." She closed her eyes and imagined Patrick's face, smudgy with chocolate—his grass-stained knees and the gap between his bottom teeth.

The rat scurried closer again. She seemed to notice Liza's sudden change of mood. "Is something wrong?"

"Yes," Liza confessed. "Something is very wrong. You see, I'm looking for my brother. That is . . . I'm looking for my brother's soul. I mean to say . . ." She sucked in a deep breath. She found it difficult to speak the words, particularly since she was speaking them to an overgrown rat in a wig and paper hat, but she didn't see what other choice she had. "I mean to say that I am looking for the spindlers' nests."

The rat let out a tremendous yelp, jumped forward, and clapped a furry paw over Liza's mouth. "Shhh," she hissed. "You must be very careful. Very careful about saying their name Below."

Liza jerked away, spitting out the taste of dirty fur, which reminded her, unpleasantly, of her aunt Virginia's mixed-meat pie.

"So you know of the spindlers?" she said.

The rat worried her tail anxiously between two paws. Her large black eyes darted nervously back and forth. "Of course I know of them. Everybody knows of them." She scrutinized Liza for a moment and then, seeming to come to a decision, leaned closer, so she and Liza were practically whiskers to nose. "It is very difficult," the rat resumed, in an anxious voice, still watching Liza intently. "Very hard to know nowadays—sides and spies. Spies and spindlers—everywhere, everywhere."

Liza felt a chill. "Please," she said. "Do you know

where the spindlers make their nests?"

The rat gave another yelp when Liza said the word *spindlers*. Then she shook her head. Then she nodded. Then she shook her head again, a motion that transformed slowly into another nod.

"Well, which is it?" Liza cried. Even now, she could feel seconds pooling and running away from them. "Yes or no?"

The rat started to speak, and then clamped her mouth shut. Then her eyes bulged, and her cheeks filled with air, as though a word was ballooning behind them. Finally she burst out, "Yes! I know, I know!" Instantly, in a flurry of agitation, she whipped out a small compact and began furiously dusting her face with powder. "Stupid rat," she muttered. "Stupid, stupid. Always muddling and messing." She shook her head. "Oh, no. No, no, no." By now a cloud of powder was swirling all around them, like a faint snow.

"Please," Liza said desperately. "I'll do anything!"

The rat stopped. She looked at Liza warily. For a moment Liza saw something flashing behind her eyes—a look of need, or greed. "Do you mean it?" the rat asked, watching Liza closely. "Anything?"

Fear made Liza's throat swell closed, so instead of speaking, she drew an X over her heart, as she and

Patrick always did when they were vowing to each other.

The rat stared at Liza for a second longer. Finally she said, "All right. I will take you there." Then, in a flash, the rat whirled around and scurried off.

Chapter 5

THE TROGLOD MARKET

Liza had not yet had time to remark on the strangeness of the world she had fallen into. The stone beneath her feet had, she saw, been deliberately carved into a wide, even path, and painted with various instructional signs.

THIS WAY TO THE MARKET!!! was written several times, in large, urgent cursive. Liza had the feeling that the words were shouting at her, an impression only furthered by the addition of several enormous arrows pointing the way.

Other painted messages cluttered the path.

BROWSERS ON LEFT; BUYERS ON RIGHT was one, as was NO BITING, KICKING, BARGAINING, OR STINGING. Another one, this time painted in ominous black, read: THIEVES, SHOPLIFTERS, NITPICKERS, AND MISCREANTS MUST APPEAR BEFORE THE JUDGE IN THE COURT OF STONES.

"This is the way to the spindlers' nests, isn't it?" Liza asked anxiously, hurrying to catch up to the rat.

"Shhh." The rat whirled around, nearly whipping Liza in the face with her tail. "What did I tell you about speaking their name?"

"I'm sorry." Liza took a step backward, alarmed by the intensity of the rat's expression. "I just want to make certain that—"

"No way to the nests but through the market," the rat cut her off, and then turned and once again scampered ahead.

All around them were clusters of the strangest houses Liza had ever seen. She knew they were houses because they were fitted with doors and chimneys. But not a single home was taller than her shoulder blade, and all the buildings were assembled of a motley collection of random materials: birdcages and soup pots, bread baskets and cookie tins, all twisted and reassembled and patched back together.

She was touched by the care with which the homes were kept; in front of one house was a well-swept

43

welcome mat; in front of another was a flowerpot half the size of the front door, in which an enormous purple flower was growing. Many of the houses were decorated with curling wisps of colored paper, giving the impression that they were all sprouting multicolored skins.

"Who lives here?" she asked the rat wonderingly.

"Who do you think? The troglods, of course. Ah, here we are now, see? The troglod market. Most of the best finds will have been snatched up by now. Still, there might be a few goodies and goodlies left."

They had turned a corner and arrived, suddenly, at a large square. Looking at it, Liza's first feeling was a dizzying sense of free fall.

The vaulted stone ceiling soared upward, like the massive arched top of a cathedral; distantly, lanterns winked among the covering of glossy purple ivy like faraway stars, filling the square with soft white light.

In the center of the plaza was a fountain carved from stone. Liza was not sure what the statue was supposed to represent: It looked like a series of animals grappling with one another, although it was hard to tell, because over the years the stone had begun to wear and chip away in places. But she definitely made out the head of a beaver; and underneath it, she thought she saw the head of a rat. At the very top of the fountain, a carved creature that looked like a cross between a bird and a butterfly was posed, mouth open, expelling a light spray of water that fell in a graceful arch into the fountain's large stone basin.

All around the market square, different booths had been assembled, again from a hodgepodge of materials, like the houses Liza had just seen, and these, too, were covered with various strips of colored paper.

But that was not what made Liza dizzy.

The vast market square was full of rocks, and all the rocks were *moving*.

Liza blinked. No—not rocks. They were small, round, rock-shaped creatures, with cracked brown-and-gray hides, nubby arms and legs, large, winking black eyes, and drooped noses that looked like very wrinkled baked potatoes. There were hundreds of them, many carrying wire baskets, or burlap sacks, or lunch boxes nearly half their size, which they were using as makeshift grocery carts.

They pushed and jostled and called to one another. The square was filled with a swell of different voices: some as low as a growl, some like the sound of a fluted high note. The din was tremendous; it made Liza's head pound.

"Troglods," she said.

45

The rat adjusted her crushed paper hat and nodded. "Very smart, the troglods," she said sagely. "You
know what they say: Never try to cheat a troglod! It's
like trying to outsniff a sningle. Now follow me, follow me. This way, please, this way."

As Liza and the rat began pushing their way
into the market square, Liza saw that the cloth rags
papering the booths were actually signs. SOCKS FOR
FIVE PURPLES! said one. NEW PEN CAPS, THREE FOR A
YELLOW! said another. Liza could hear, too, snatches
of individual conversations.

"Outrageous! Last week it was one green for a
key, and now they're trying to charge me a blue!"

"Tin cans for a bargain! Two reds gets you two
cans!"

"Don't you try to tell me this sock doesn't have a
hole in the heel! Do you take me for a dingle-bat?"

"What's all the colored paper for?" Liza said.
Despite her anxiety, she couldn't help but be curious.
Everywhere, troglods were exchanging small slips of
colored paper: reds, blues, greens, and purples. Some
of them looked to have been cut away from cardboard cereal boxes or greeting cards; others looked
like scraps of wrapping paper.

The rat stared at her in amazement. "You didn't
think the market was *free*, did you?" The rat shook her

head. "Personally," she continued, "I've never understood why the world Above is so crazy for green. Absolutely mad for it!" The rat dropped her voice again. "I've always been a fan of pink. Very rare, of course . . . very hard to come by . . . extremely valuable . . . the troglods would give up their houses for a half-dozen pinks. . . ."

"But—" Liza was going to point out that in her world people used real money, not just worthless slips of paper, but it occurred to her that she wasn't actually certain of the difference, and so she said nothing.

"Get your bottle caps! Get your bottle caps! Two reds and a bargain at that!"

"Batteries! Used batteries, right here! Best in the market!"

As they moved through the market, a few troglods shot her a curious look, but most of them continued bustling on their way, squabbling and bargaining, picking over the booths—which were, Liza saw, filled with all the little nips and bops that always seemed to get lost: stray socks and old keys; lipstick tubes and sunglasses; used Post-it Notes and packs of gum.

Liza remembered what her father had once said: *Glasses don't just get up and walk away by themselves.* And it was true. The troglods were walking away with them. She realized, with a jolt, that

everything she had mysteriously lost over the years—
her sheet of butterfly stickers in second grade, her
favorite crystal barrette, the locket she had inherited
from her grandmother—might very well have ended
up here, at the troglod market.

She realized, additionally, that she had seen a
troglod before. She recognized the wrinkly brown
backsides.

"There was a troglod in my yard only last week,"
Liza burst out. They were nearing the end of the market, where it was a little quieter. "I thought it was a
gnome."

The rat let out a peal of laughter. She whipped
out a handkerchief and dabbed the corner of her eyes,
which were smeary with mascara. "A gnome! Bless
you. What an idea."

"So . . . gnomes aren't real?" Liza asked.

The rat stared. "Of course they're *real*. But who
ever heard of a gnome living all the way down here?
The gnomes are northern creatures. Wouldn't be
caught dead beneath the eleventh parallel."

Liza felt warmth flare in her stomach. So Anna
had been right about the gnomes—they *did* like the
cold.

But that meant she had probably been right about
the spindlers, too. The warmth drained out of her at

once. She thought about the last time she had asked Anna what on earth the spindlers needed souls for— how Anna's face had gone paper-white, how her eyes had gone blank and frightened, like someone suffering from a bad shock. How she had shaken her head sadly, without saying a word.

The rat sensed her change in mood. "Come on," she said, and scuttled on.

Liza put a hand in her pocket and squeezed the baseball pressing into her thigh. And even though she was not Above, and was not standing with her face in the fir tree, she allowed herself to make a wish.

This one I will tell you:

Please, please, please. Let me rescue Patrick in time.

Chapter 6

Liza

THE LUMER-LUMPEN

They moved into an area of dense forest. All the trees were covered in layers of thick, green moss, as though they were draped with fuzzy blankets. The air smelled like wet, new earth, and Liza saw large, jewel-colored butterflies flitting through the trees. It was clear, however, that the path was well-traveled. Above their heads, the same pale, glowing lanterns were nestled among the canopy of vine- and moss-covered branches, which reminded Liza of long fingers encased in green woolen gloves, knitted tightly together.

Every so often, the rat would stop abruptly,

remove a cracked pocket mirror from her lunch box, and stare at her own reflection, while Liza danced impatiently behind her and bit back the urge to tell her to move on.

Once the rat produced a tube of lipstick, which she slathered liberally over her pink lips, whispering, "Just a little more color . . ." Another time she removed a small makeup compact—Liza would have sworn it was one her mother had lost only a few weeks earlier—and patted and pouffed her face until she looked as though she had gone face-first into a snowdrift.

With every minute that passed, Liza had a harder time controlling her impatience. Finally she couldn't stand it any longer. "Excuse me," she said. "I don't mean to be rude, but—but—"

The rat blinked at her expectantly. Her black eyes looked even darker above her powder-white nose.

Liza faltered under the rat's stare. "I mean it hardly seems necessary—when we're on an urgent mission . . ."

"*What* hardly seems necessary?" the rat asked coldly.

"What I mean is . . ." Liza gestured helplessly at the rat's outfit.

"Is there something the matter," the rat asked,

her gaze growing fiercer, "with the way that I am dressed?"

"I just . . . well, it isn't natural, is it?" Liza sputtered.

Instantly she knew that the rat had been offended. The animal drew herself up to her full height.

"Natural!" the rat exploded, with such volume that Liza drew back, and several butterflies flitted nervously away from the path. "And what, little miss, do you know about natural? Is it natural to be forced to sneak and slither in the corners, and skulk in the shadows, and dig for your meals in Dumpsters?"

"Um . . ."

"And is it natural for people to hurl shoes at your head, and try to snap you in traps, and stomp on your tail?"

"I—I guess not. . . ."

"And is it *natural*," the rat thundered, quivering with rage, "for some to be cuddled and coddled and hugged, while others are hated and hunted and hurt, because of differences in fur, and tail, and whisker length? I ask you—is *that* natural?"

"I'm sorry," Liza said, desperate for the rat to calm down. They needed to keep moving, and above all, she did not want the rat to abandon her.

"I only meant that—you know—I've never seen a rat dressed up before."

"Oh, yes? Is that so? And when was the last time you *looked*?" Now, alarmingly, the rat's eyes began to fill with tears. She withdrew her white handkerchief from her lunch box and began blotting her eyes. But it was no use: Globs of mascara began running down her cheeks, matting her fur and making her look even more hideous than ever. "When was the last time you actually *spoke* to a rat, instead of shrieking and jumping on a chair, or poking it with your horrible broom?" And with a final sob, the rat spun on her heel and started to move off.

"Hey," Liza said. It was now her turn to become offended. "It's not all my fault. Rats never speak to *me*, either."

"And why should they?" The rat whirled around to face her again. "Why should they come near you at all, when you are only going to poke them with your broom?"

"That's absolutely ridiculous," Liza snapped, finally losing her temper. "I've never poked a rat with a broom in my whole life."

"But you've thought about it, haven't you?" the rat pressed.

"No, I haven't."

"Not even once?"

"No!"

"Not for a second? Just a quick bop over the head?"

"No—never—not once!" Liza dug her nails into the handle of the broom.

"Aha!" the rat crowed triumphantly. "You're thinking about it now!"

"Fine!" she burst out. "Fine, yes! I could bop you over the head; I could poke you in the eyes; but only because you're the worst, most irritating, most impossible rat I have ever met in my entire life!"

Just then, and all at once, the glowing lanterns went out, plunging them into perfect darkness.

Instantly Liza's irritation was transformed to fear. "What happened?" she cried. "What's going on?"

The rat clucked her tongue. "Dear, dear. Now you've gone and upset the lumpen."

"The *what*?" Liza's heart thudded hard in her chest. She was not exactly afraid of the dark—but then, she had never been in dark this dark before. She couldn't make out her hand in front of her face, or even the shape of the rat, who she knew must be standing only a few feet away from her.

"The lumer-lumpen. The light-bearers. They're very sensitive—don't like a lot of mussing and fussing."

The rat sighed. "I suppose we'll have to apologize. We can't very well go on like this. Not with those useless eyes of yours—just like a pair of stones, aren't they?"

"My eyes aren't useless," Liza protested.

"How many claws am I holding up?" the rat said. Of course Liza had no idea, so she gripped the broom and remained silent. The rat tittered. "See? I told you. All human eyes are useless. You see only what you expect to see, and nothing more; and what is the use of sight like that?"

Liza thought about saying that up until thirty seconds ago, she had been staring directly at a giant rat in a newspaper skirt, which was assuredly a sight she had *not* wished to see. But she needed the rat's help, infuriating though the animal was. And Liza was used to squashing down her feelings. So she said nothing at all.

"But it is too dark in here—far too dark, yes," the rat continued gaily. Then she turned and called out, into the long tunnel of darkness, "Can we get some light, please?" Her strange voice echoed and rolled into the blackness. "We'll be as quiet as church mice and as grateful as gidgets!" Then the rat whispered to Liza, "Although, of course, church mice aren't really quiet at all. They're the *most* awful gossips."

For a moment they stood there.

"Is something supposed to happen?" Liza asked after a short pause.

The rat sighed again. "Infuriating creatures— truly. Overly sensitive, if you ask me, and with no sense of the changing times. The formality they require . . ." Then the rat trumpeted out, "Illuminate, elucidate, bring forth the light; for friends, or strangers, and those seeking sight." She added, in a murmur, "I always feel so silly saying that."

Suddenly the lanterns began to glow again, and Liza exhaled. Unconsciously, she had been holding her breath.

"Better?" the rat asked, watching Liza with her black eyes narrowed.

"Much better." Liza was immensely relieved.

The rat spoke to her once again in a whisper: "For all their airs and demands, they really are extremely useful. Yes; yes; very useful."

"Who're they?" Liza asked. She was by this time convinced that the rat was—despite seeming friendly enough—quite deranged.

The rat blinked at her. "The keepers of the light, of course. The lumpen." And she pointed to one of the small, glowing lanterns suspended directly above their heads.

For the first time, Liza noticed that curled at the very bottom of the glass dome was a tiny, pale, crescent-shaped thing, faintly glowing.

"Oh!" she cried out, delighted, because she saw that this tiny figure was the source of the soft, pale white light. "A glowworm!"

The lights above them flickered dangerously.

"Shhh!" the rat hissed. "The light-bearers go only by their official name—the lumer-lumpen. They're *extremely* sensitive about titles," she added in an undertone.

"I didn't know that glo—um, lumpen were sensitive about anything." Liza strained onto her tiptoes to get a better look. The glowworm certainly didn't look sensitive, or easy to offend. In fact, it didn't look as if it would feel much of anything at all: It was a small, pale lump, totally inert.

The rat scoffed. "That is a common misunderstanding about the lumpen. They are supposed to be very unfeeling—some would even say cold. But believe me—they are *extremely* sensitive. All geniuses are, of course."

"Geniuses?" Liza repeated doubtfully, still staring at the whitish lump.

"Prodigies! Geniuses! Artists! The lumer-lumpen are some of the most sensitive, the most brilliant, the wisest creatures on the earth or inside of it. There is more wisdom in the head of a lumpen than you will find in all the libraries of the world."

Liza refrained from pointing out that from what she could tell, the glowworm did not even *have* a head. Its head and bottom appeared to be entirely indistinguishable. She wondered whether this would affect the quality of its thoughts—if, in fact, it had any.

"If they could only speak," the rat continued, and Liza was alarmed to see that tears welled up in her eyes again, "the secrets they might disclose to us! The wisdom they might impart! The stories they might convey! That is the source of their light, you know. Excess brainpower." The rat shook her head wonderingly.

Liza's head was spinning; she did not know what to believe. On the one hand it seemed incredible that such a tiny, ugly, bulgy little grub could possess any power of thought or feeling; on the other hand, she was standing in a dark tunnel with a rat wearing a skirt and lipstick, so she supposed that really, anything was possible.

She advanced several paces down the tunnel,

craning her neck so that she could stare up at the glass domes nestled in the canopy of mossy green branches above them. In each of them, she now saw, was nestled another tiny glowworm, a crescent no bigger than a fingernail clipping, glowing and pulsing with light.

"How many are there?" Liza asked. "How far do they go?"

"Oh dear. Dear me. There are ever so many lumpen, thousands and thousands. You can always count on them to light the way, remember that. These tunnels are full of twists and turns, and it is easy to get lost. But the lumer-lumpen always light the path. They know all the ins and outs. Yes, thousands of them. In fact, they go almost all the way."

"Almost all the way *where*?" Liza said. She was having trouble keeping up with the rat's excited babble.

"To the spindlers' nests, of course," the rat said, dropping her voice reverentially on the word *spindlers*. For a moment, as she passed directly underneath one of the lumpen's lanterns, her eyes glittered a brilliant violet color. "Hip-hop and top-tip and look smart about it. We've still a very long way to go. And I expect we'll want to be in and out before the Feast begins, won't we?"

Liza's heart stopped. "The . . . the Feast?" she repeated.

The rat looked nervously from side to side. "The Feast of the Souls. Surely, you've heard . . . ?"

Liza was filled suddenly with a coldness that froze her voice completely. She could only shake her head.

The rat lowered her voice to a whisper. "Well, they need to eat, don't they? Hungry, that's what they are. They want control—power over everything Below."

"But—" Liza found her voice. "But that's terrible. We have to stop them."

"Ah." Once again, the rat's eyes flashed momentarily violet, and for a second a look of sadness passed across her face. "But there will be no stopping them once they feast, my dear. No stopping them at all. All the world Below—everything you see—will be theirs for the taking."

Now she understood why Anna had always been so terrified when Liza asked her about the spindlers and what they did with the souls of the children they took.

They feasted. They grew fat and powerful.

Liza's fear turned to resolve. "Don't you know any shortcuts?" she asked desperately.

The rat paused, seeming to consider it. "I suppose

we could cut through the palace grounds. . . . Although the nids won't like it. . . . It's nearly time for the nightly ball, and these days it's invitation only."

"The nids?" Liza repeated uncertainly. She was not at all sure she wanted to meet any more underground creatures.

"*Silly* creatures, if you ask me." The rat sniffed. "Still, I suppose they have a right to their fun." Then she paused, cocked her head to one side, and listened. "What did I tell you? Just on time! You can hear the music now."

It was true: Suddenly Liza *could* hear music. Faintly, delicately, like the sound of bells and wind through the grass and distant flutes, all woven together. It seemed to be coming from somewhere on their right, and before Liza could protest, the rat had plunged into the mossy forest and started toward it.

Chapter 7

Mirabella

THE PALACE GATE

As they pushed farther into the dense forest, Liza had more and more trouble keeping up. The vines seemed to snake around her feet, and the branches to snatch greedily at her vest. She tried to use the broom to clear a path, but even so she found herself stumbling, and whiplashed by thorny bushes.

The rat chanted, "Slowpoke, slowpoke," over her shoulder, for the fifteenth time in two minutes.

Finally Liza couldn't stand it anymore, especially since she was moving as fast as she could. "Excuse me," she said as she dodged a low-hanging branch, which was encased in a thick green shag of mildew. "I have a name, you know, and it isn't *slowpoke*." Her courage faltered somewhat as the rat turned around and stared at her beadily. "You can call me Liza."

The rat stopped walking. "Oh, pardon me, *Miss* Liza. I didn't mean to offend," the rodent cooed, giving a quick curtsy. "And I suppose it has never occurred to you to ask me for my name, even though here I am, scuttling around to lead you to where you are going?"

"I—I—I—" Liza stuttered.

"I suppose you didn't even think I might *have* a name?" the rat huffed.

"Well, I—I mean—" The truth was that it had *not* occurred to her that the rat would have a name.

"Hmph. I thought so." The rat regathered her tail around one dainty wrist before flouncing off.

"I'm sorry," Liza said. The rat only sniffed. She was scampering more quickly than ever; Liza had to jog to keep up. "I'd like to know your name. Really, truly," Liza said. "Cross my heart and hope to die and stick a needle in my eye." She made a little X over her heart, and felt a small pulse of pain as she thought of Patrick.

She remembered how he had once said to her, after a bad nightmare, *You won't let the spindlers get me, will you, Liza?* And she had said, *Cross my heart . . .*

The rat abruptly stopped walking. Liza stopped too, panting a bit.

"Mirabella," the rat said, in her throaty, squeaky way. "My name is Mirabella."

"That's a beautiful name," Liza said grandly, even though she thought it was a very odd name for an overgrown rat in a straggly skirt, wearing a grubby wig on her head.

The rat leaned in a little closer. Her breath smelled of wetness and dirt, and Liza tried not to wince. "I came up with it myself. I had to; the other rats don't believe in names. Everything is so *uncivilized* down here."

Liza curtsied deeply, staking the handle of the broom in the ground to balance herself. "Very pleased to meet you, Mirabella," she said. "Liza Flavia Elston, at your service."

The rat looked almost ecstatic. She pinched two strips of newspaper carefully between two long, yellowed claws and mimicked Liza's gesture. "The pleasure is all mine, Miss Liza."

"There." Liza straightened up, laughing. "That's all right, then. You don't have to call me 'miss,' though. No one ever does Above."

64

"Above . . ." A look of deep longing came over Mirabella's face. She leaned forward, until her whiskers were nearly poking into Liza's cheeks. "Tell me," she said. "What is it like to live Above?"

Liza was taken aback. "What do you mean?"

"The sun," Mirabella said, clenching and unclenching her paws. "What is it like to bathe for hours in the sun?"

"Um . . ." Liza had never really thought about this before. "I'm not really sure how to describe . . ."

"Is it as hot as the space between a wall and a furnace?" Mirabella asked. In her excitement, her tail had once again become unraveled from her arm and lashed wildly against the ground. "As steamy as a sulfur pit? As warm as a slop pot?"

"Um . . ." Liza struggled for words. It was funny, she realized, how she had never thought about it before. "It's like being wrapped in a nice blanket," she finally said.

"Ahhh, a blanket," Mirabella said wistfully. "I once had a blanket—found it in the Dumpster behind St. Mary's School. It was very nice, almost like new, except for the big burn hole in its center and the smell of sardines. Yes—a very good blanket. I lost it, though, in a bet with a badger." Mirabella frowned. "You mustn't think I'm a gambler, of course, not regularly.

But sometimes when the worm races are on . . . And I suppose your mother tucks you up all nice and neat every night when you go to sleep, doesn't she?"

Liza was having trouble following the dizzying twists and turns of the rat's conversation. "I—well—I mean, not really. She used to. She doesn't so much anymore." Liza remembered that when she was very little, her mother had liked to sit on her bed at night and tell her stories, and even sing her little songs. That was Before: Before the exclamation point made its permanent home between her eyebrows, Before she had become so tired all the time, Before the stacks and stacks of bills. Liza was not sure what had changed, but something had, and she thought it was very unfair.

People were not supposed to become different. Things were supposed to stay As They Were.

Mirabella leaned forward once more and whispered conspiratorially, "I have always dreamed of having a mother."

"But surely you have a mother," Liza said, extremely surprised. "Everybody does."

The rat rocked back on her heels and waved a paw. "Oh, yes, in *name* I have a mother, of course. Rat 2,037. That's what they call her, among the Tribe. But with seventy sisters and brothers, you can hardly expect that she'd have time for me, oh no. Besides, the thirty-seventh is her favorite; all because he was born with a perfect nose for sniffing out rare steak."

"Seventy!" Liza exclaimed. She didn't know what she would do if she had seventy sisters and brothers. She had difficulty enough just looking after Patrick.

"My mother is very busy," Mirabella said. "I have seen her only once or twice since I have been grown. No, no. I mean a real mother: a mother to cuddle you and hold you and kiss you when you have fallen down." The rat was growing more and more agitated. "A mother to smother you with kisses! And coddle you with care! And squeeze and squinch and squelch you in hugs!"

"Yes—um—I guess I see what you mean," Liza said. She found it slightly alarming when the rat grew so energetic, partially because she did not want Mirabella's long nude tail whipping around in her direction.

"Can I tell you a secret, Miss Liza?" Mirabella asked.

"Of course," Liza said.

Mirabella cupped her paw to Liza's ear, and Liza tried as hard as she could not to pull away, though in truth the feel of the animal's matted fur—and hot breath—disgusted her. "I have never been hugged."

Mirabella drew back, looking ashamed, as though she had just confessed to killing someone.

"Never?" Liza couldn't help but feel sorry for the rat.

Mirabella shook her head, her bottom lip quivering ever so slightly. Liza prayed she would not begin to cry. "Never ever," Mirabella said, in a wail. "And I have dreamed . . . but who would want to hug a rat? Who would cuddle and coddle me, and tickle my ears? Rats are *dirty*, and *filthy*, and *diseased*; they're *garbage diggers* and *bad-luck bringers*." It was obvious, from the way Mirabella spat out the words, that she had heard these insults many, many times.

"The most we can ever hope for is a broom in the eye," Mirabella said. She whipped out her small golden compact and began furiously repowdering, creating such a storm of makeup that Liza could barely contain a sneeze. "Now if I had been born a cat," Mirabella said, "it would be a different story. Oh, yes. A far different story. Cats, with their round little eyes and their tiny little noses and their cute, cuddly tummies and tails! Fine animals! Precious little things! Ha!"

Mirabella abruptly turned and scampered forward once again into the thick network of fuzzy-mitten trees. Liza hurried to follow, and caught her toe on an enormous root that was protruding from the ground. For a moment she was falling, and then the broom went clattering from her grip, and then she landed on a pillowy pile of dark undergrowth.

Liza sat up. Her pajama bottoms were now coated in green muck. Her mother would kill her. Liza let out a very small groan.

Strangely, the forest groaned in response: a sound that soon swelled to a roar.

The trees began to shake, and creak; and then, all around her, the tangle of branches began slowly to separate, like a jigsaw puzzle coming apart. And as the trees, like crooked fingers, straightened and withdrew, a narrow carpet of trimmed green moss was revealed, running toward a dazzling palace that seemed, from a distance, to be made of light. At the same time, the music surged in volume, as though it had previously been muffled by the mess of wild growth.

Liza gaped. Mirabella let out a titter of laughter.

"How absolutely silly of me," she said. "Here I was, gabbing away—and I almost entirely missed the palace gate. Come along now, come along."

Chapter 8

Nids King

THE DANCE OF THE NIDS

"It used to be that the balls were open to everybody," Mirabella explained, as she hurried down the long green alley toward the palace. "The gates were never closed—not for hundreds and hundreds of years. Anyone and everyone was welcome to come and dance! Moles and nids, toads and tripoli. Even rats! Yes, yes. Even poor scruffy rats like me were allowed to attend."

"So what happened?" Liza asked. She was trying very hard to listen to Mirabella and to memorize everything she was seeing: the trees, now dignified

70

and perfectly straight, that lined the path on either side; the topiary bushes, trimmed to look like different animals; the dozens of lumpen nestled in the glossy tree leaves and glowing like tiny Christmas lights strung among the branches.

Mirabella glanced around nervously. "It's the spindlers," she whispered. "Never know who's on what side and which is playing for who. It's made everybody anxious, you know. Now the nids are nids and the moles keep with the moles and the tripoli don't hold truckle with anyone. Members only—orchestra and nids alone. And there is no more dancing for the rats, oh, no."

"This is a shortcut, isn't it?" Liza asked anxiously.

Mirabella gave her an injured look, and only sniffed in reply.

They were nearing the palace, and Liza could hardly keep from gasping. It appeared to be made of crystal, or quartz. Carved out of the translucent rock were an enormous series of pink and white spires and winding outdoor staircases, dazzling ramparts, and high towers. The palace stretched vastly upward, high as the highest skyscrapers Liza had ever seen or imagined—and in every corner, and on every peak and winding balcony, were more lumpen, lighting the palace with a dust-rose glow.

71

The music was even louder now. It was the strangest music Liza had ever heard: It seemed to be made of gasps and whispers, and babbling-water sounds, as well as of stringed instruments and high, fluting voices.

"Now let me see, let me see . . . ," Mirabella was muttering. "If we just cut around the palace, we'll be a hop, skip, and a jump from the River of Knowledge, and from there we shouldn't be far from the Twin Mountains. . . ."

As they began skirting around the palace, the music swelled louder. Its strains reached out and wove themselves around Liza, freezing her in place.

Come closer, the music seemed to say. *Come dance.*

It was as though it had reached inside her and was tugging her toward the palace; unconsciously, she moved across the soft moss carpet toward the enormous vaulted palace windows. "Just a quick look," she said, more to herself than to the rat.

The windows were low enough that she could easily peer through them without straining onto her tiptoes, and they were made of the thinnest, prettiest glass Liza had ever seen—pink-tinged, like the rest of the palace walls, and full of bubbles and imperfections that slightly distorted the view of the palace inside.

And what a palace it was. It took Liza's breath away; it made her insides ache, as though the music had just plucked the core of her, like a string.

The hall stretched vastly into the distance and was carved with so many ornate surfaces and mirrors, it made Liza dizzy to look at. There were pale white branches in beautiful crystal vases arranged at intervals along the floor, in which hundreds of lumpen were resting, filling the hall with a soft, golden light. The ceiling was actually a vast and complex system of roots, which had been whittled and polished until they shone like dark amber.

The orchestra was clustered on a raised platform directly in front of the window to which Liza had pressed her nose. Liza blinked several times, and then pinched herself, to make sure she had not accidentally gone to sleep and begun dreaming.

But no. She was not dreaming. The maestro, a mole, was directing an orchestra of bullfrogs and crickets, hummingbirds, and one very large, very grumpy-looking animal that Liza thought might be a badger.

The mole stood on a chair, gesturing broadly with a baton. It was dressed elegantly in pants and coat-tails, which were so long they pooled on the floor. All the animals were dressed elegantly, in fact, although

the crickets wore nothing but top hats perched rak-
ishly on their heads, and the effect of the frogs' outfits
was somewhat ruined by the fact that they were spotted with moisture.

The crickets sang; the hummingbirds beat their
wings against tiny bells; the frogs croaked out a rhythm;
and every so often, the badger sang out a great, deep,
throaty roar, which intermingled with the other notes
perfectly and sent a shiver up Liza's spine.

"Beautiful, isn't it?" Mirabella whispered. Liza
jumped; she had not realized that the rat had
approached the window. Tears welled up in the rat's
eyes. "I've always loved this piece. It reminds me of
the days . . . but no matter, no matter. Things are
different now."

"Where are the nids?" Liza whispered back. "I
don't see any."

"Oh, they'll be along shortly," Mirabella said.
"The party's just getting started. See? Here comes the
master of ceremonies now."

"The master of ceremonies?" Liza pressed as
close to the glass as she could; she wished she could
pass directly through it and into the beautiful room,
and dance and sway with the music. Dimly she was
aware of a rhythm drumming through her: *Patrick,*

Patrick, Patrick, it said. But the rhythm of the hummingbirds and crickets drowned it out quickly and swirled Patrick's name into her subconscious.

Mirabella said in an excited whisper, "Look! See? He's climbing the stairs."

In one corner of the gigantic room was a golden staircase that spiraled toward the ceiling. Mounting the stairs in a very dignified way was the smallest person Liza had ever seen. At first she thought it must be a child; but as she squashed her nose even farther against the window, she saw that the person had a luxurious, sprouting beard that hung shaggily around his deeply lined face, almost like a cat's fur. He was simply no taller than a toddler. His hands and fingers were, on the other hand, extremely large.

"A nid," Liza breathed. Her breath fogged the glass in front of her, and she swiped it away quickly with a fist.

"Not just any nid," Mirabella whispered. "A royal. Only kings and queens can preside over the dance."

As he reached the top of the staircase, the king of the nids cleared his throat and raised both arms.

The mole maestro made a sweeping gesture with

its baton, and the orchestra fell totally silent. Liza found herself holding her breath.

"Let the dancing begin," the king said in a high, reedy voice. Instantly, in response to his command, the ceiling glittered with thousands of flickering lights.

Liza stifled an instinctive cry. Her first impression was that the ceiling had caught fire. Then she saw that the shifting, mobile pattern of blinking, blazing lights was, in fact, made of fireflies: Thousands of them floated across the ceiling, arranging and rearranging themselves among the polished roots in dazzlingly complex patterns.

The orchestra burst into a triumphant, joyful waltz, and the doors at the far end of the vast room were flung open as nids began to stream into the ballroom, chattering and laughing, as above their heads the roots continued to glow and sway and let off showers of sparkling color.

Now Liza saw that the king was, comparatively, quite tall. Most of the nids would not have reached higher than her knee, and all of them—including the women—had soft-looking, red-whiskered faces. They wore tunics that seemed to be made of moss and cobweb, and as they spun and twirled across the room, Liza felt as though she was looking through her old kaleidoscope at the dizzying array of swirling colors.

The dancing was as beautiful—no, *more* beautiful—than the music. She had an irrepressible urge to get closer, to join in the celebration. The toads, increasingly excited as the music switched from a waltz to a jig, began hopping up and down, periodically blocking her view of the dance floor.

Liza darted to the next window, where the view was better. She barely heard Mirabella calling her back. Her ears were filled with the rhythm of the music and the drumming of all the nids' tiny feet against the floor. The window was very slightly ajar, and it was hinged like a door, so it opened into the room.

If Liza just poked her head in—just for a second— she would have a view of the whole ballroom. . . .

"Miss Liza! Miss Liza! Be careful!"

Liza placed one hand very carefully on the window and eased it open a few more inches. . . .

Suddenly a red-whiskered face popped up directly in front of her.

"Intruder!" the nid trumpeted. "Trespasser! Stranger! Gate-crasher!"

Liza tried to pull back, horrified, but the nid grabbed her wrists and tugged her headfirst into the room. She toppled forward, somersaulting in the air, and landed on the palace floor on her rump. The broom was ripped from her hand. Now everything was a chaos of thin, piping voices.

"Intruder! Intruder! Intruder!"

Nids swarmed her, tugging her hair and sniffing her shirt, poking her with long, pale fingers.

"What is it?"

"How *ugly* it is."

"Where are its whiskers?"

"Is it a giant?"

"It isn't a giant. It's a human child. Can't you *smell* it?"

"Leave me alone!" Liza cried out. She tried to push the nids away, but there were too many of them. There were hands all over her now, hauling her upward, heaving her into the air. She was on her back, gripped by hundreds of iron-strong fingers, flailing. "Mirabella! Help me!"

"Miss Liza! Grab on to my paw!"

Mirabella had appeared at the window, looking pale and desperate. Liza tore an arm free of the nids' grip and tried to reach for Mirabella's extended paw. The nids wrenched them apart, so Liza came away with only a handful of brownish-gray fur.

"Mirabella!" Liza screamed, but already the nids

had swelled forward and had grabbed the rat firmly by the shoulders. They hauled Mirabella into the room as they had done to Liza, then heaved her into the air above her heads, plucking the ruined hat from her head and picking at her wig.

"Let go of me!" Mirabella shrieked. "Get your filthy hands off my hair! Stop fiddling with my skirt. I—ow! *That was my tail!*"

The nids paid no attention to their protests. "A rat and a monster!" they chattered excitedly. "Strangers and intruders! Criminals in our midst! They must be punished!"

The orchestra continued playing, but now the notes were frenzied and discordant. Directly above her, the fireflies were flitting ever faster around the vaulted ceiling of roots. Now Liza found their movement frightening, as though the ceiling was covered with golden-skinned snakes.

They passed underneath the golden staircase, where the king of the nids was standing with a finger pointed toward the double doors, through which the nids had come. "Criminals must be punished!" the king thundered, and the nids cheered. "Intruders must be educated! Strangers must be abolished! *Bring them to the Court of Stones!*"

"The Court of Stones! The Court of Stones!" the nids chanted.

"Oh dear," Mirabella squeaked as they were carried through the double doors and swallowed up by darkness.

Chapter 9

Judge Gobbington IV

THE COURT OF STONES

The nids carried Liza and Mirabella down a broad set of stone stairs into a dank, dark part of the palace, where slicks of black mold clung to all the walls, and the only light came from a few dim clusters of sick-looking fireflies straggling through the air. As they passed through dark caverns, Liza could hear the lapping of water from up ahead, and fear snaked like a cold, damp finger down her back.

"Please!" Liza cried out, renewing her attempts to fight the nids off. Now that she had shaken off the fog of the music, terror came rushing in its place:

Patrick's name drummed louder than ever in her mind. "Please let me go. You don't understand. I'm on a very important mission."

"Save your breath, Miss Liza," Mirabella said in a low voice. "You'll need it for the Court of Stones."

The finger did another unpleasant zaggle down her back.

The nids set Liza and Mirabella down at the edge of a vast, fog-enshrouded lake. The surface of the black water was spotted with enormous, dark flowers, which looked like overgrown teacups. As soon as the nids reached its shore, the flowers began to move, skating toward them, leaving behind a gentle wake of dark ripples.

Then Liza saw that the blooms were being pushed upward from underneath; and suddenly dozens of large, slimy green frogs were waddling up through the shallows and plopping down on the banks on their fat, wet stomachs, blinking expectantly. Each frog had one of the oversize lily pads strapped to its back, and Liza found herself pushed, headfirst, into one of them.

She managed to grab hold of one of the flower petals and right herself. Immediately Liza's frog waddled back into the lake. Her stomach dipped as all at once it submerged. But the flower stayed above water, skating easily along the surface. Around her, the water was alive with floating flowers, sliding rapidly toward the opposite shore as though moving on invisible tracks. Wisps of mist floated past them.

Liza wished, fiercely, that Patrick were with her. She remembered when, the summer before, he had found a large frog in the creek at the bottom of their street, and how they had tried to hand-feed it lettuce before Sarah Wilkins had walked by and sneered at them both for being freaks. Liza should have stood up to Sarah. *The* world *is a freak,* she should have said. *Everything that happens in it is strange and beautiful.*

Liza felt a hot flash of fear and guilt. What if she didn't make it to Patrick on time? Who would play Pinecone Bowling with her then? Who would tromp through the woods with her on summer days, and build snow forts with her in winter, and try to water-bomb Mr. Tenley's snarling, drooling bulldog from the tree house?

They reached the opposite shore quickly. Liza saw what looked like a ruined castle rising up from beyond the mist. Scattered lumer-lumpen pulsed dimly along its black stone ramparts. Liza's throat squeezed up. She wished she could plunge her hand into the water, grab on to the frog, and instruct it to turn around.

But all too soon it had waddled onto the shore.

I am not afraid, Liza told herself. *I am not afraid.*

"Get down," commanded the nid that had stolen her broom, and thrust the bristles threateningly in Liza's direction.

"Only if you stop sticking that thing in my face," Liza said, surprised that she sounded very much in control of herself. The nid withdrew the bristles several inches from her nose, and Liza climbed, with some difficulty, out of the flower and maneuvered down to the ground with as much dignity as she could muster. Mirabella, looking somewhat green in the snout, slid down from her own flower and bumped onto the soggy ground next to her.

As though in response to the nids' arrival, the door to the castle groaned open, and Liza came face-to-face, or face-to-snout, with a large mole very much like the one that had been in charge of the orchestra. This one, however, was wearing a floppy, faded nightcap, which looked as though it had been fashioned from a used coffee filter. In fact, it most *certainly* was a used coffee filter; Liza caught a whiff of hazelnut as the nids prodded her forward. She bet he had gotten it at the troglod market.

"Come along, come along," the mole said, turning

on one furry heel and leading the way into the dark palace. "We heard you coming from a mile away—could have woken a slothbart with your screaming! The court is already assembled. Had to wake up the judge, and I'll have you know he was not pleased, not pleased in the slightest. . . ."

"The judge is known to be very strict," Mirabella whispered to Liza, and Liza's stomach turned.

The corridor opened up into a vast, semicircular amphitheater chiseled from dark stone. It looked like the baseball stadium at Fenway Park, but thousands and thousands of years old. Hundreds of tiers of blackened stone seats were arranged in a semicircle, stretching endlessly upward, and Liza saw a smattering of sleepy-looking troglods and other creatures—including a skunk, still wearing a tattered bedsheet around its shoulders—which had apparently gathered to watch the trial.

Beyond the open amphitheater, Liza saw a river, which swirled with strange colors, opals and blues and deep purples, and emitted a vivid blue light. The river, Liza thought, must also be causing the strange shadows that flickered and floated and flew all around her.

"Sit!" the nid with her broom commanded, pointing Liza toward a rickety wooden bench. She regretted having brought the broom with her at all. It was getting very tedious to be poked and prodded by the bristles, and she began to sympathize with Mirabella's great fear of the things.

Liza took a seat on the bench. Mirabella sat down beside her. They were sitting directly in front of a wooden podium; Liza guessed this was where the judge would sit, when he—or she, or it—arrived.

Mirabella was very nervous. She was worrying her tail between her paws, muttering, "Oh dear, oh dear, oh dear."

"Stop that," Liza whispered. "You'll make us seem guilty."

The rat moaned.

"Shhh," Liza hushed her. "Pull yourself together. Everything will be okay. I'm sure the judge will understand that this is all a big mistake." Liza wished she felt as confident as she was pretending to be. She cursed herself for listening to the nids' music, for getting close to the palace at all. It must have been hours since she'd descended Below; and if what Mirabella had said was true, the spindlers' Feast would soon begin.

The nids filed into the stone seats that encircled the court, buzzing and chattering excitedly. Almost as soon as the nids were seated, the mole cried out,

"All rise for the Honorable Judge Gobbington IV!" Instantly there was shuffling and rustling, and murmurs of excitement, as the nids climbed again to their feet.

Liza stood along with everybody else. Mirabella was practically white with fear, and Liza's throat was dry and chalky, as though she had inhaled sawdust.

She heard a scuffling sound, the noise of slapping footsteps along the dark, dank hall through which the mole had led them, then a dry, rattling cough. Finally the judge stepped into the amphitheater.

At least, Liza thought he must be the judge. He certainly looked wise. Although he was probably no taller than she, his head was four times the size of hers and incredibly wrinkled, like an enormous, shriveled pea. His face, in contrast, seemed ridiculously small: just a bare twig of a nose, and two squinty eyes, and a pinched mouth floating in the middle of that humongous head. Liza felt the wild urge to laugh, as she did sometimes when she got very nervous, and fought desperately to quell it.

Judge Gobbington IV had a large gavel tucked under one arm. He was wearing thick glasses and an elaborate black gown that reached almost all the way to the ground. His bare feet protruded from underneath its hem, however, and Liza saw that they were large and slightly webbed, like a duck's. When he walked, his feet made a wet, slapping sound against the stone.

Still, despite his faintly absurd appearance, the judge moved with solemn confidence, like someone supremely aware of his own importance. As he mounted the podium, Liza whispered to Mirabella, "What—what is it?"

Before the rat could respond, the judge shot Liza a withering look. "I see you are a stranger to the world Below," he said in a reedy voice. "Otherwise you would surely be familiar with the Gobbingtons. We were the first family of hobgoblins to settle this region, back when the lumpen were still young and the nids were no more than nobs in the ground—when flowers had not yet learned to grow, and water and land did not know that they were separate." Judge Gobbington IV frowned. "You would *also* be familiar with the fact that hobgoblins have excellent hearing. I trust you will not make that mistake again."

"N-no, sir," Liza sputtered. She sank back down onto the bench, and her heart sank with her. Obviously, she was not off to a very good start. The nids began tittering again, whispering to one another as they reseated themselves.

The hobgoblin judge banged loudly with his gavel on the podium to restore order. "Now, then," he said. "What's all the fuss about?"

The nid with Liza's broom stepped forward. "Your Honor!" he cried. "The rat and the human child were snooping and spying! They were lurking and leering, and peering and prodding—"

"You've made your point quite clear," the judge snapped, with another thunderous *bang* of his gavel. The nid shrank back, picking nervously at the broom's bristles.

Judge Gobbington turned his attention back toward the bench. He slid his glasses down on his small, pinched nose and stared at Liza over the top of them, as though she was an expired piece of deli meat in a refrigerator and he was trying to determine whether eating her would give him a stomachache. It was, she thought, very unpleasant to feel like a slice of spoiled turkey. "Let's hear what the defendants have to say for themselves."

Liza swallowed, and opened her mouth. But before she could speak, Mirabella burst out, "Your Honor, this is all a terrible mistake!" The rat sprang to her feet, frantically trying to smooth down a few curls of her dirty skirt. She looked even more pathetic than usual. Thick gobs of mascara streaked her cheeks, and her whiskered chin was trembling. "We got lost, you see, on our way to the troglod market—"

"Don't listen to the rat!" came the shrill voice of another nid in the audience. "Everyone knows that rats are liars!"

"And fools!"

"And foolish liars!"

The courtroom exploded into sound, as the nids began babbling and firing accusations at Mirabella and Liza in turn. Mirabella sank to the bench with a little squeak of misery. Her ears burned bright pink.

"Order!" Judge Gobbington banged his gavel against the podium, trying to quiet the ruckus. "I said, order in the court!" But if anything, the nids only got louder.

"Please!" Liza burst out. She was struggling to be heard over the chaos of voices. "Please!" she tried again, with no effect. She took a deep breath, stood up, and tried a third time. *"Please!* Listen to me. I'm running out of time. I'm only here to rescue my brother. His soul has been stolen by the spindlers."

As soon as she said the word *spindlers*, complete and total silence fell on the court, except for a few stifled gasps from the audience.

Judge Gobbington IV put down his gavel. He stared hard at Liza for several seconds, and she forced herself to remain standing, and balled her hands tightly so he wouldn't see they were shaking.

"What do you know about the spindlers?" the judge asked in a hoarse whisper.

"I—I don't know anything about them," Liza said. The sudden silence was even more nerve-racking than the eruption of noise. "I know that they're bad. I know that they have my brother—and, and, that they're planning to take over everything Below. And I know I have to stop them."

"And you came Below all by yourself?" the judge asked incredulously.

"I *was* by myself," Liza corrected him. "Mirabella agreed to help me. She agreed to take me to the spindlers' nests." There were more gasps. Liza turned and gave Mirabella a small smile, but Mirabella was once again working her tail between her paws, muttering, "Oh dear, oh dear, oh dear."

The judge removed his glasses. Without them, his eyes were no larger than two small raisins set in the vast floating balloon of his head. And yet, Liza felt she could see herself reflected endlessly inside them.

"And you will risk your life in the nests," the hobgoblin said, "and pit yourself against the queen of the spindlers, to save your brother?"

Liza swallowed. The way Judge Gobbington IV

said it made her plan sound both foolish and hopeless. "Yes," she croaked out.

The judge leaned forward. "Why?"

Liza had not expected the question. She opened her
mouth and then closed it again. It was, she realized, a
difficult thing to explain. Images of Patrick swirled in
her head: Patrick toddling behind her through drifts
of snow on their way to skate across Gedney Pond;
Patrick all sneezy and sleepy with allergies, dozing
next to her in the car on long trips to the Adirondack
Mountains; Patrick elbow-deep in mud, trying to
gross her out by finding worms; Patrick scanning the
yard for gnomes or standing lookout at the riverbed
for Sarah Wilkins and her group of snotty, snooty
friends.

"Because . . ." She couldn't put any of her feelings
into words. *Because he's my brother,* she thought of
saying. Or, *Because he would do it for me.* What
came out was: "Because I have to."

"A likely story!" a nid erupted from the audience.

"*'Because I have to!'* What kind of a defense is
that?" cried another nid.

"She's a spy, I tell you! Both of them are slippery,
nippery, nasty little spies!"

Liza balled her fists again. She felt anger rising in her chest, pushing at her throat. Next to her,

Mirabella had begun to rock back and forth. She was clutching her head so tightly, it made her cheeks bulge out from between her paws. If Liza hadn't been so upset, it would have been comical.

"I'm not a spy," Liza said loudly over the din. "And I'm *not* a liar."

"Order, order!" The judge was pounding his gavel once again. "In the name of the authority vested in me by the Court of Stones, I declare the defendants *guilty* by reason of insufficient proof! And proven inefficiency!"

On the word *guilty*, Liza's heart stuttered. For one second, time seemed to stop, and stretch, so that she could think of her mother and father, and Mrs. Costenblatt in her rocking chair on her porch, and feel sorry that she would never see them again.

And poor Patrick . . .

Liza was filled with regret. She had forgotten to tell the real Patrick, her baby brother, so many important things. For example, she had forgotten to tell him that when you reached third grade the cafeteria would try and give you celery and peanut butter with raisins on top and pass it off as dessert, and how important it was *not to be fooled*, and instead stuff your pockets with gummy bears before school. She had forgotten to tell him too that the last time they had played Chesteropoly she didn't let him win, as she said she had, but had in fact been beaten by him fair and square.

Then time jumped forward again, and everything was uproar and chaos.

"To the dungeons!" the nids squealed as they poured from their stone seats and flowed down to the courtroom floor. "Throw them in the dungeons and leave them to rot!"

Liza found herself surrounded by the jabbing, chattering creatures. She realized she must fight, or be left to rot in the world Below forever. The nid with the broom poked at her again, and she managed to snatch it from his grip.

"Stay away from me!" She turned in a circle, jabbing threateningly at the nids that came too close. "Or I'll bonk you over the head, and sweep you out the—oof!"

A nid jumped on her back and brought her tumbling to her knees. Mirabella was engaged in her own struggle, fighting and snapping and using her tail as a whiplash to try and keep the nids away. But there were too many of them.

"To the dungeons!" The nids' voices swelled to a roar. "Lock the spies in the dungeons!"

Then suddenly there was a rushing, fluttering

sound, like the first pitter-patter of rain falling onto pavement, swelling quickly into a downpour. Instantly the nids fell silent. Liza managed to wrench her arm away from the nid that had been holding her. Even Judge Gobbington IV had gone ghostly white.

"Wonderful," Mirabella squeaked in a tone of deep sarcasm. "*Now* see what you've done? You've gone and upset the nocturni."

Chapter 10

THE NOCTURNI

Thousands of shadows were swooping and flitting through the air above their heads, until the court was dark with them.

But they were *not* shadows, Liza realized as she looked at them more closely. That is, they were like shadows—they had the bare, thin, flickering, insubstantial quality of shadows—but unlike shadows, they were all the same shape. There were hundreds of thousands—no, millions—of them, and they were all about the size of Liza's palm. They looked like butterflies, except that they had the long, pointed beaks

96

of hummingbirds, and they seemed to be made out of darkness and air.

There was a rustling, as thousands of quiet voices spoke in unison.

"Release the rat and the human child," the nocturni said, and their voices sounded like dry leaves tumbling over one another.

"You heard them," the judge croaked out. "Release the defendants at once."

Liza found herself released. Instantly the nids began to withdraw. As they backed slowly and cautiously out of the court, they tittered anxiously, scanning the air above their heads and muttering various apologies at the floating, flitting shapes.

"A mistake! A mistake! Happens to the best of us."

"No intention to offend . . ."

"A harmless little prank . . ."

"Very sorry, of course, won't happen again . . ."

Soon Liza and Mirabella were left alone with the swirling black nocturni.

"Well," Mirabella sniffed. "Well." She patted her wig, parts of which had become hopelessly tangled. "I hope you're happy. I told you to stay away from the nids. And now they've taken my purse. . . . If it hadn't been for the nocturni . . ."

"The what?" Liza turned a full circle, stunned,

all the while keeping her eyes on the drifting shapes above their heads, like a dark snow.

Mirabella muttered something that sounded to Liza like *useless* and *humans* and *heads as empty as a beggar's purse*. At a normal volume, the rat said, "The nocturni." She shot another reproachful glance over her shoulder at Liza. "Lucky they decided to speak up, or we'd no doubt be rotting to a pulp in the dungeons by now! Like forgotten bananas. Like turned cheese!"

"Are they—are they dangerous?" Liza swallowed hard, thinking of the fearful way the nids had fled from them.

Mirabella dropped her voice to a whisper. "*Very* bad luck to displease the dream-bringers," she murmured. "*Very* bad luck. I once knew a badger . . . oh, but we won't speak of him. Terrible, terrible. Spends his days counting socks at the troglod market . . . convinced that the nocturni are sending messages to him through the color patterns . . ."

"Dream-bringers . . ." Liza repeated. She didn't know exactly what Mirabella meant, but she liked the sound of it. "There are so many of them."

"One for every person in the world," the rat replied.

"No." This stopped Liza short. "It's not possible."

The rat whirled around, clearly growing impatient. "Of course it's possible," Mirabella said. "It's *necessary*. You didn't think the nocturni would share, did you? There is a nocturna for every single person in the world! And each night the nocturni sip dreams from the River of Knowledge, and fly out into the world, and deliver them to their humans."

"So . . ." Liza struggled to understand what Mirabella had just said. "So I have a nocturna of my own?"

"You, the bus driver, the grocery store clerk . . . The nocturni mate for eternity. Even after you die"—the rat's voice dropped to a hush—"your nocturna will never take another human, not for all the length of time in the universe and beyond. Your nocturna is wedded to your soul. Some even say"—the rat paused again, chewing on her lower lip with her pointed front teeth, and coating them with lipstick in the process—"that it is the nocturni who carry souls into the Shadow World when we die, where they will watch over them and keep them safe forever. Some say that is nocturni's ultimate purpose."

Liza shivered. The cavern was cold, and full of shifting light. The underworld, she thought, was strange and beautiful and frightening, like the nocturni themselves.

As she looked at them more closely, she realized it was not true that they were all shaped identically. They were all roughly the same size, true, and all possessed that same insubstantial dark quality, but she noticed that the wings of every nocturna were slightly differently, with ragged tips that formed special individual patterns, almost like snowflakes. And for the first time, what the rat had said—a nocturna for every single person in the world—struck her, and made her feel temporarily breathless. It was unimaginable.

Patrick had a nocturna. That was not so strange, actually. His dreams were crazy and full of weirdness, and she was not surprised to learn that he had had help coming up with him—where else had that dream about the chickens running a marathon come from?

But her father, too, and her mother! That they dreamed at all was a revelation. She had always assumed, in some way, that they powered off at night, like computers, and booted up again in the morning, with a whole new series of downloaded complaints and annoyances and problems and irritations. She could not begin to imagine what they would dream about. Taxes, perhaps . . . ?

Suddenly her mind was skidding over all the people she knew and trying to comprehend that single, stunning fact: They, too, had dreams.

Wings fluttered above her, no two quite the same. *Yes,* she thought, *just like a black snow.* She unconsciously lifted her arms, as she used to stand in the rain when she was very little, enjoying the tickly feeling of the water coursing over her skin. And after only a moment, the nocturni responded. They began swirling and whirling lower until they surrounded her entirely, and as they did the sounds of their wings— the humming and fluttering that echoed through the cavernous space—took on a kind of rhythm.

Suddenly the rhythm became speech, and Liza could hear little babbling words being beaten into the air by the motion of the wings. There were so many voices flapping toward her at once that she could only isolate certain words and snatches of phrases: "down the corner," "bake shop," "elephant wearing a top hat," and it took her several minutes to realize that the nocturni were babbling happily about the dreams of their humans.

Then Liza noticed a nocturna hovering closer than all the others. It stayed in constant motion, circling her shoulders, swooping up and down around her head, a black, fluttering blur. As it did, its wings beat out a funny, staccato voice, which seemed to Liza somehow familiar. It was like the stuttering rhythm of her heart when she was very excited.

No—it *was* her heart; the voice was coming to her through the rhythm of her own heartbeat.

She noticed, now, that the other nocturni were withdrawing, falling silent, drifting upward into the murky blackness.

"Are you my nocturna?" Liza said out loud, and thought she could detect a faint tittering from the mass of nocturni above her. They were laughing.

She heard repressed laughter, too, in the voice of the nocturna still circling her endlessly. *You don't have to speak out loud, Liza,* it said. *I can hear what you're thinking.*

No way, she thought immediately, and the voice pushed back.

Of course.

So you're my nocturna?

Yes.

Liza thought about this. *Then you've known me my whole life?*

Again came the rustling, fluttering laughter, like a pitter-patter in her heart. *Far longer than that.*

Do you have a name? she thought.

Yes. There was a temporary pause. *But it's long, and very difficult to translate into human language.*

Try, Liza thought.

There was another moment's pause. The nocturna hovered close to Liza's chest; she could feel it there, parceling the air, like a small and concentrated wind. Then images began rising through her, one after another: a flash of sunlight on silvery water; spinning clouds of reddish dust; explosions of bright color; lava hardening into black stone; a flower unfurling its petals, coated in sparkling dew; lightning tearing across a purple, cloud-clotted sky; a child laughing.

The images stopped, and Liza was left breathless.

That's your name? she asked.

Part of it, the nocturna said.

Mirabella had been watching Liza closely, her nose twitching. Now she scurried closer to Liza. "It's very special," she said. "Very, very special. Humans don't get to meet their nocturni."

She wished she could stay with the nocturna. She felt reassured by its presence. It was even more comforting than the broom, which she still carried tightly in one hand. But she knew they had to move on. She no longer knew how long she had been Below, but she knew they were running out of time.

I have to go, she said regretfully. *I'm on my way—*

To save Patrick, the nocturna finished for her. *I know.*

You know about Patrick?

Of course. I know everything about you. The nocturna whirled a little faster. *Follow the river upstream and take the road that leads through the Live Forest. It's a shortcut. But be careful not to wake the trees.*

Okay. She knew, immediately, that her nocturna could be trusted.

Good luck, Liza, it said. *We'll be watching.*

"Thank you," Liza said out loud. Nothing but echoes came back to her; and so she and Mirabella continued on their way.

Chapter 11

Mirabella

THE LIVE FOREST

They followed the river upstream, as Liza's nocturna had instructed them, and Liza found herself captivated by the water that babbled happily on their right. She had never seen water that looked so . . . *alive* before, so full of motion and color.

And now she could hear, too, that its sounds were not just regular water sounds. Beneath the babbling and the gurgling and the flowing, she thought she could make out other noises: voices, and high laughter, and the ringing of bells, and a woman—or more than one woman?—singing in a rich, warm voice that made her think of honey, and other golden things.

Without meaning to, she drifted closer and closer to the edge of the water. The farther she moved along its banks, the more she was filled with the overwhelming desire to look into the river, to put her hand in the water.

No. She wanted to swim. She wanted to be completely submerged.

Suddenly Liza felt a pressure around her middle and was tugged backward; the rat, using her tail as a lasso, pulled her sharply away from the river.

Liza's feet flew out from underneath her and she landed, hard, on her elbows and tailbone, barely managing to keep hold of her broom. Pain zinged through her.

"What are you doing?" she cried out, as the rat uncoiled her tail from around Liza's waist and wrapped it, once again, around her wrist. "I could have broken something."

"You could have done much worse than that," Mirabella said. "Much, much worse. You must stay away from the river at all costs."

"I only wanted to look," Liza said. She sat up, feeling her elbows tentatively for swollen places.

"That is exactly what you must never, ever do," Mirabella replied solemnly, offering Liza her paw.

Liza refused to accept it. She climbed to her feet slowly, on her own.

"Why not?" she asked. There seemed to be a lot of rules to the underground; almost as many as there were in the world Above. No doubt—if she ever made it back—her mother would ask her how she came to get so many bruises, and if Liza told her the truth, she would get in trouble for making up stories.

Liza felt a pang. It felt like days since she had passed through the cavernous hole in the basement. She wondered whether Above, her mother and father were frantically trying to find her. Would they think she had been kidnapped? Would they think she had run away?

"The River of Knowledge is for the nocturni alone," the rat said. "They drink from it, and it sustains them. But to everyone else it is deadly."

Liza cast one last, regretful look at the river and allowed the rat to lead her on. Soon they entered a place of heavy growth, where vines climbed thickly up the gnarled trees that surrounded them, and formed a canopy overhead. In places even the river was blocked from view, obscured by luscious growth, all of it in colors Liza had not seen before in any garden—black and dark purple and silver. Occasionally she saw a flower so white and huge, it reminded her of the moon. The light of the lumer-lumpen pulsed among the thick growth. Several butterflies, dark as velvet, flitted between the vines, causing the leaves to stir.

Occasionally she heard rustling, and the sound of tiny feet scrabbling through the growth on both sides of them; she tried very hard not to imagine what kind of creatures lived in this huge, black forest underground. Once she thought she detected a large, furry body shifting to her right. Her heart seized in her chest, and she was terrified to look and terrified not to; when she did, she saw two oval eyes blinking at her. The animal retreated just as quickly, and the eyes folded back into the darkness, but not before she caught sight of a long, thick pink tail, like an enormous worm. Another rat: She would have sworn to it. She wondered if Mirabella had seen.

So as not to be frightened, she thought of Patrick— not the fake-Patrick who lay aboveground, sleeping soundlessly in Patrick's bed, but the real Patrick, who would put his warm arms around her when she told him about everything she'd done to rescue him, and listen with his mouth gaping open, and say things like, "No way," and "Uh-uh," and "Impossible," so that she could squeeze him back and say, "Yes, of course."

That was what her parents did not understand—and had never understood—about stories. Liza told herself stories as though she was weaving and knotting an endless rope. Then, no matter how dark or terrible the pit she found herself in, she could pull herself out, inch by inch and hand over hand, on the long rope of stories.

They reached a gloomy, gray space in the forest. Huge, twisted trees—dead trees, as far as Liza could tell, with not a single stem or bud or branch that bloomed—spiraled into the mists that swirled above them.

The trees were larger than any Liza had ever seen in her life. She seemed to be standing, in fact, among their roots: vast, vaulted arched roots that reared out of the earth before looping back into it again—like a series of monstrous, deformed arms—and formed tunnels underneath and around the ash-gray wood. She could hardly make out the trunks that soared above them, but each was the circumference of a house.

A weathered sign staked crookedly was marked with ghostly white letters: THE LIVE FOREST, it said. ENTER AT YOUR OWN RISK. Beyond the sign were two paths. One path was well swept and made of neatly cobbled stone, painted an inviting cream color and lit by what looked like ornate streetlamps—except the lamps were tall, white birch trees, and the lightbulbs were dangling lumpen, glowing within their translucent domes. This path veered sharply to the left and followed the periphery of the forest the long way around.

The other path was just a bare space beaten into the dust between the dead-looking trees, and it went straight into the heart of the Live Forest, vanishing after only a few feet into the gloom.

Liza recalled what her nocturna had told her: *Follow the river upstream and take the road that leads through the Live Forest. It's a shortcut.*

"Well, well." Mirabella chattered nervously. "Sometimes it's better to beat around the bush, don't you think?" The rat scurried onto the well-lit path.

"Wait!" Liza swallowed. There was an evil feeling to the Live Forest, and she had no desire to walk through it. But the nocturna had said it was a shortcut. "It'll be quicker to cut through the forest."

Mirabella let out a mangled squeak. "*Through* the forest? Surely you don't mean . . . you're not suggesting . . ." She swallowed. "The Live Forest is a place for spooks and evil spirits. Very bad luck. *Very* bad luck."

"We have no choice," Liza said. "Now come on."

She took two steps along the crooked path, attempting to look brave. Instantly the mist engulfed her, as though she had been swallowed by a slick, damp throat. "There's nothing to be afraid of."

Mirabella patted her wig nervously. "For the love of cheese . . ." she said, but she scurried along after Liza.

Liza squinted. There was a bit of pale white light that descended from above—from where, she could not have said, as they must have been miles and miles underground—just enough to make out the enormous silhouettes of the trees, and the mist clinging to them like moss.

The gnarled roots rose on all sides of them. Liza felt like a ship moving among large, glittering icebergs. It was the strangest thing: Even though the forest was perfectly still, with not a solitary shred of movement anywhere—just the terrible gnarled trees and the heavy, motionless mist—Liza still had the uncomfortable feeling of being watched.

Liza thought back to the nocturna's instructions. The nocturna had said to take the path through the Live Forest. . . . And it had said something else, too. Something important. . . .

"Now let me think," Liza murmured. "Watch out for the trees? No, no. It was something else."

"What's that?" Mirabella whispered.

"Be quiet. I'm trying to think." It *was* something about the trees, though . . . she was sure of it. . . .

"You're buying a sink?"

"I said I'm trying to think."

"You're eyeing a mink?"

"I'm *trying* to *think*." Liza whirled around, losing patience. Mirabella had been creeping so close to her, they were practically whiskers to nose, and the rat hopped backward with a startled yelp. Her tail got entangled with her feet, or her feet became entangled by her tail, and suddenly she was stumbling backward. She pinwheeled her arms but could not regain her balance. She tumbled down at the base of one of the looming tree roots, bumping her head against the ancient wood.

"Mirabella!" Liza cried, and ran to her, dropping to her knees. "Are you all right?"

The rat's wig had slid forward so it obscured one of her eyes. She was rubbing her head and moaning.

"My head!" she cried. "My tender, pulpy head!"

Then the rat froze. Liza froze too. Suddenly, from all around them, came the low sounds of rumbling, as of distant thunder: cracking, too, and beneath it all, a horrifying, sibilant hiss.

"What is that?" Liza asked. All the fear had slammed back into her at once. The ground was rumbling and rolling beneath their feet, as though an earthquake was building. "What's happening?"

But even as she asked, the nocturna's words came back to her.

You mustn't wake the trees.

At that moment the root—the dull, gray, lifeless root that had bruised Mirabella's head—shook itself and began to twist, and uncurl.

And uncurl.

And uncurl.

It extracted itself from the ground with a terrible tearing sound and raised itself in the air, and at its tapered point was the mossy, dirt-encrusted face of a grinning, wood-colored snake, with shining black eyes and terrible gray fangs.

The tree snake stared at Liza, swaying lightly on its enormous coils. Every time it moved there was a cracking sound, as of a giant crashing through a forest, and Liza watched in horror as little bits of bark flaked off from its skin.

"Run!" Mirabella screamed, and became a streaking comet of fur, rocketing past her.

But Liza couldn't run. She was so terrified she

couldn't move, or breathe. Her whole body was filled with leaden weight.

The tree snake reared back, and the hissing sound in the air grew louder. A dark forked tongue flickered dangerously in its mouth, and Liza knew the snake was about to strike.

At that instant, the tree snake lunged for Liza, lightning quick. She barely had time to roll out of the way before the snake had plunged its fangs into the space where she had been kneeling, driving its mouth into the dirt. She bumped hard up against another tree root, and this one began to shake and crack as well.

Liza scrambled to her feet, holding tight to the broom, filled with blind panic. Around them, other trees were uprooting themselves violently, and from everywhere. All over the forest, the tree snakes were wrenching themselves from the ground, coughing up dirt. They loomed through the mist, their bark rippling terribly, sometimes three or four of them radiating in a circle from their trunks, like monstrous pets leashed together.

"Liza! This way! Follow me!" Mirabella was scrabbling ahead, weaving a path through the sway-ing, swirling forest and all the living, deadly trees. For once she had forgotten about walking like a lady and was running on all fours.

Another tree snake lunged for Liza, and she sprang out of the way, feeling a whistle of wind on her neck as the snake snapped its mouth on air. It came at her again. She struck out frantically with her broom, and the tree snake clomped down on the bristles, so Liza was left with only the handle. The snake coughed out a mouthful of straw, giving Liza just enough time to scamper out of its reach. It strained for her but was pulled back, sharply, by the tree trunk at its center; it gave a dissatisfied hiss as Liza plunged blindly forward.

"This way, this way!" Mirabella was digging frantically in the soft earth, sending sprays of dirt pinwheeling out from beneath her paws. At every moment, even more tree snakes were waking. The cracking and hissing was almost deafening, the ground buckled and shook beneath them, and the air was a shower of bark, pattering down from above like a black rain.

Then Liza's world turned a cartwheel; pain slammed her blindingly from the left, and her feet were above her head and her head was skimming several feet over the earth, and it took her a full 3.7 seconds to realize she had been knocked off her feet. The patch of ground she had been standing on had cleaved suddenly and completely in two, opening up like a book upon which she had been perched; she was seesawed into the air and landed, hard, on her back. The air went out of her at once, and in those moments of breathlessness everything appeared to move in slow motion.

From out of the cleft in the ground rose, inch by inch, a coal-black head the size of a car. It emerged from the earth as if it were floating up through water—the most fearsome snake Liza had yet seen, dark and rotten, encrusted all over with dirt. Its fangs were looped with smaller brambles, and insects skittered out of its mouth; moss grew along its bark and down its chin, a long, tangled beard. It glowered at Liza, hissing, and its breath smelled terrible, like death and long-buried things.

Liza wanted to stand. She wanted to run. But her brain no longer seemed to send clear directions to her body. Her body was possessed by terror; her lungs had stopped working; she couldn't think.

The black snake hissed at her again, taking its time, sending a forked tongue through terrible cracked wooden lips. It shimmied a few feet closer, its ancient body snapping and cracking: a deafening noise echoed through the forest, and all the other tree snakes fell silent, watching. Somehow Liza knew that this was the oldest tree of all, the center of the Live Forest—its longest and largest root, and its meanest, evilest snake.

Then the snake struck. It lashed out without warning, and Liza saw nothing but a tunnel of black about to consume her. Instinct took over, and she rolled desperately to one side. The snake's fangs whizzed by her; she could feel a *whoosh* of air as its massive body missed colliding with hers by inches. She jumped to her feet. She could breathe again. The blood was pounding through her, her heart churning furiously.

"Liza! Over this way!"

Only Mirabella's head was visible, her snout protruding over the lip of a hole she had excavated in the dirt. Liza took off running as the snake lunged for her again. She turned around, flailing out blindly with her broom. She struck the snake in the eye, and it reared back, roaring with fury. Just four more feet and she would slip down into Mirabella's hole and then maybe, maybe, the snake would not be able to get them; just three more feet.

Behind her, the snake let out a screech. Liza saw its shadow swallow hers, and she knew it was headed for her again. She felt its hot breath on her heels, on her neck, on the crown of her head. . . .

"Jump, Liza!" Mirabella screamed.

Liza dove headfirst. She felt a sharp pain in her left heel, and then cold air, as the snake clamped down on one of her sneakers, yanking it off her foot. She was flying; she was falling; then she was colliding with Mirabella and tumbling into the narrow dirt tunnel, head over paw over hand over claw, landing in a pile of matted fur and dirty newspaper.

"Mirabella?" Liza whispered as the rat let out a moan. "Are you okay?"

"Get—off—me," Mirabella wheezed. "Can't breathe. On—my—stomach."

"Sorry." Liza disentangled herself from the rat. The tunnel was so narrow and low she had to crouch on her hands and knees, and she felt very much like a rat herself. Ahead of them was a solid wall of dirt; the rat had not had time to dig very far. "Now what?" Liza asked.

"Plan A! Plan A! We wait," Mirabella said. In the dark, her eyes glittered. "We wait for the trees to tire themselves out and go back to sleep."

"Do you think we're safe here?" Liza shivered. From above, they could still hear the horrible sounds of crashing and cracking, hissing and roaring.

"Oh yes," Mirabella said, but Liza did not think

the rat sounded entirely sure. "Very safe. Safe as a bug in a rug. Safe as a clam in a turtle shell. Safe as a needle in a haystack!"

"I don't think—" Liza started to say.

But she did not get to finish.

At that moment the black tree snake came crashing its way into the tunnel, lashing and snapping.

Mirabella screamed.

And as the mouth of the snake loomed over them, an enormous, black vaulted mouth hung with moss and coated with black and slimy things, Liza did the only thing she could think to do. She reached out with all her might and shoved the broom handle deep into the snake's throat.

The snake stopped, mouth gaping open, its fangs only an inch from Liza's neck.

It blinked at her.

She held her breath.

And then the snake began to cough. The broom handle had lodged itself sideways in the snake's throat.

The tree was choking.

"Mirabella," Liza said in a low voice, keeping her eyes on the snake the whole time. It was now twisting and turning its massive neck, trying to work the broom out of its throat. And the second it did, Liza knew, they would be snapped up like mice in a trap. "I'm not sure waiting here is the best idea."

"No, no. No. We mustn't wait any longer. Very *unsafe* here," Mirabella squeaked nervously. "We must move on to plan B."

"What's that?" Liza shuddered in the blast of hot, foul, musty air that emanated from the tree snake's mouth. A beetle dropped from one of its fangs onto her thigh, and she brushed it off quickly, pushing herself backward in the tiny, narrow tunnel.

"We dig," the rat said.

Chapter 12

Liza

THE SEEDS OF HOPE

Mirabella burrowed through the soft earth, and Liza helped her, scooping mounds of dirt with her hands. They crawled forward foot by foot, placing more and more distance between themselves and the tree snake, which still choked and coughed and wrestled with the broom handle lodged in its throat.

Liza was glad she did not have a fear of small spaces: On all sides, she was being squeezed by packed dirt, and she was constantly bumping her head, and her knees were scraped up from banging over small stones buried in the earth.

The heat and the hard work began to fray Liza's nerves, and Mirabella's temper.

"You're stepping on my tail again."

"I'm not stepping on anything. I'm crawling."

"Then you're *crawling* on my tail."

"It's not my fault. It was nearly poking me in the eye before."

"It wouldn't poke you if you would give me space!"

"There *is* no space."

When Mirabella judged it safe to angle the tunnel upward, they ascended toward the surface and emerged at the far edge of the Live Forest. As Liza crawled out of the tiny tunnel, shaking dirt from her pajama bottoms, she took long and grateful gulps of air.

Behind them, the trees of the Live Forest had once again gone to sleep, cocooned in mist. It was almost impossible to believe, even now, that in their roots slumbered the terrible snakes.

"Well, now," Mirabella said, suddenly cheerful again, as she brushed the dirt from her newspaper skirt, which had become quite hopelessly tattered. Only a few panels remained, and tufted bits of fur from her large, thick hind legs protruded between them. It was strange how once you saw a rat wearing clothes, it became slightly disgusting to imagine the animal naked. "That wasn't so bad, was it?"

Liza stared, speechless.

"What I wouldn't give for a mirror! And a little bit of rouge! I'm sure I must look awful right now—a mess. A frightful, frazzled, fizzled mess!" The rat adjusted her wig—which had begun to slip dangerously toward her chin—and blinked expectantly at Liza.

"Oh! Um—n-no. Not at all," Liza stammered politely, even though the rat looked even more ridiculous than ever. Dirt was mixed with the powder and the mascara now, so her face appeared to be two wholly different colors, and a pebble and a small twig were caught in her wig.

As they went on, the ground beneath them turned hard and gray and was punctuated by areas of gravel and large, jagged rocks. They had lost sight of the river, although Liza thought at times she could detect echoes of its strange babblings. She noticed that they had begun to wind upward; then the mist before them cleared and she saw vast boulders rising up in front of them, and a narrow path cutting through the rock.

"It's—it's a mountain," Liza stuttered out. And it was: so many rocks layered on top of one another, forming a series of peaks. Of all the amazing things she had seen—Mirabella, the nocturni, the nids, and the tree snakes—this struck her as the most incredible. A mountain, Below!

"Mountains," Mirabella corrected her. She had already started scrabbling up the path. "There are two of them—the Twins, they're called. From here we must be very careful," the rat added, lowering her voice. "We're close to the border of the Bottomland: spindler land. From here, everything belongs to the queen, and to the Valley of the Lost Souls, where the spindlers have made their nests. There are spies everywhere. We must go like shadows—like shades—like dust!"

Liza nodded to show she understood.

"Well, come on, then," Mirabella said. "Up we go, to the tippy-top. No point in gaping and gaggling."

The path they followed was no wider than two steps and must have been infrequently traveled. In some places it was no more than a faint impression of displaced stones, and in other places it disappeared altogether and they had to scramble over the large, flat rocks that jutted out of the foothills. Occasionally Mirabella stopped and—alarmingly and without warning—dropped flat to the ground. The first time this happened, Liza cried out, thinking that the rat had been injured; she ran to help, before discovering that Mirabella had only pressed her nose to the ground and was sniffing furiously.

"That way!" Mirabella pronounced, springing to her feet and straightening her wig, which had begun to skew dangerously to one side. She confided in a whisper, "When in doubt, follow the feet! Sniff for the toes! That's what you do. Of course, once that brought me straight to a half wheel of Camembert cheese . . . made a nice dessert for the brothers and sisters that night . . ."

Up, up, up they wound, up the barren, rocky path. Liza began to be very sorry that the tree snake had eaten one of her sneakers; her socks did not protect her from the sharp stones in the path, and soon the sole of her right foot was aching. At a certain height, she began to notice large, brittle brown shrubs that grew up among the boulders. They were hung all over with thousands of tiny dark seeds—each no larger than a pinhead, and quite ugly, Liza thought.

"What are those?" she asked Mirabella, pointing to one of the scraggly bushes.

Mirabella stopped walking. "Those are the bushes of hope," she said. She removed the wig from her head and pressed it to her heart, like a person about to recite the Pledge of Allegiance. Underneath the wig, her fur was tufted in some places and matted in others. "Aren't they beautiful?"

"I guess so," Liza lied, wrinkling her nose.

"There you go again," Mirabella said miserably. "Judging a book by its cover and an animal by its tail. Go on. Look a little closer. And be lively about it." She clapped the wig back on her head and crossed her arms.

Liza bent down close to the branches and peered hard at the tiny, dangling seeds. They were teardrop-shaped and at first appeared to be a solid black, the color of onyx. In fact, other than their strange shape, they looked almost exactly like poppy seeds, which Liza did not *at all* like and which were, she thought, a perfectly good way to ruin a lemon muffin.

But on closer inspection, Liza noticed that at their very center there was a tiny bit of pure white light—this no bigger than the fine, tapered point of a needle—that nonetheless was so blindingly bright she jerked backward, blinking.

"Oh," she said, rubbing her eyes. "Oh."

Mirabella tittered. "I should have warned you. The seeds are full of light. Each seed contains as much light as your sun!"

Liza stared at her. "Impossible."

Mirabella swept her tail around her wrist and gave an imperious sniff. "That is a human word," she said. "And a very ugly one at that. We have no use for it Below."

"Bushes of hope . . ." Liza bit her lip. "Does that mean—I mean, well, does that mean what I think it means? Does that mean that these seeds . . . ?"

"Are seeds of hope, yes. Of course."

The only thing Liza could think of to say was, "They're so small."

Mirabella snorted. "Small—and powerful enough to knock your socks off. Oh yes. Strong stuff. Big as a boom!"

"I didn't think hope was something that grew," Liza said.

"Of course it grows," Mirabella said. "What else would it do? Sing?" She leaned a little closer. "The nocturni are the bearers of the hope seeds." As usual, when she spoke of the nocturni, the rat lowered her voice and looked anxiously from left to right, as though worried one of them might be eavesdropping. "That's why it's such bad luck to cross them. . . . They carry the seeds Above, and plant them in souls where they're needed."

Liza wished again that she had Patrick with her.

Everything about Below was strange and different. "Can I—do you think I could take some? Just a few, I mean?"

Mirabella waved a paw. "Take what you like," she said. "The bushes of hope grow everywhere Below. They can grow in the soiliest dirt and the rockiest roads!"

Liza reached out and skimmed her right hand along the branches. They even *felt* like poppy seeds, she thought, as the seeds quivered and came away in her hand—a dozen of them, black teardrops against her palm. She transferred them carefully into the right pocket of her pajamas, along with Patrick's socks and her father's glasses, which were amazingly intact. She could do with some hope right now. It was nearly the only thing keeping her going: hope that she would reach Patrick in time, and hope that she would not be too late to stop the spindlers.

"Patrick and I will bring some to Mrs. Costenblatt," she said out loud, because it helped to believe, truly believe, that they would go Above again. True, Mrs. Costenblatt couldn't see very well—she might, Liza thought, even try to eat them—but she would be happy with the gift even if she didn't know what it was.

"Who is Mrs. Costenblatt?" Mirabella asked.

"A friend," Liza replied. "She lives across the street."

"A friend, a friend." Mirabella repeated the word, a rapturous expression in her eyes. "What a beautiful word."

Liza shrugged. "I guess so."

"I have never had a friend," Mirabella said sadly. She began plucking at the remaining panels of her newspaper skirt, which were so coated with dirt that the print had become illegible.

"Never?" Liza repeated, stunned. "Not even one?"

Mirabella shook her head.

Liza didn't know what to say. Mirabella looked so pathetic, in her strange, sloppy wig, fiddling anxiously with her tail, Liza couldn't help but feel sorry for her. Everyone deserved at least one friend. At least Liza had Mrs. Costenblatt. And Patrick, of course. Anna would be her friend, she felt sure, if Anna would just come back from college. And Mirabella was taking her to the nests, where she would—she *had* to—rescue Patrick and the other souls that the spindlers had stolen from Above.

Liza made a sudden decision. "I'll be your friend," she announced. She had trouble speaking the words but was glad once she had spoken them. She did not really want to be friends with an enormous rat of questionable sanity, but it seemed the right thing to say.

Mirabella did not seem cheered, however. If anything, she began to worry her tail more frantically, until Liza was scared she would snap it in two.

Chapter 13

Mirabella

THE QUEEN'S SPIES, AND THE WAY ACROSS THE CHASM

The air grew cold and thin, and Liza wrapped her arms around her waist and panted cold white clouds into the air. Higher up, she and Mirabella came across groups of birds massed among the rocks.

Birds, or bats; Liza could not decide. They were as ugly as bats—large, about the size of vultures, with webbed wings, hooded eyes, and long, sharp beaks. They were white and featherless. Looking at them gave Liza an uncomfortable, itchy feeling and reminded her of standing in the front of Mr. Toddle's classroom, reciting her multiplication tables; she'd had the same feeling then of being scrutinized and evaluated.

The birds—or bats—followed Liza and Mirabella's progress carefully. As they passed among the rocks, a few of the creatures lifted off from their perches, gliding into the darkness on silent wings.

"She knows we're here now," Mirabella said in an excited whisper, watching the enormous bird-things circling above them.

"Who's she?" Liza asked.

"The queen of the spindlers," Mirabella said, and Liza felt a zip of anxiety run up her spine. "The moribats keep watch for her. Spies, secret-spillers, and tattle-tellers—that's what they are."

"Shouldn't we hide?" Liza asked.

The rat tutted at her. "No way to hide from the moribats. Nothing happens Below that the moribats don't find out about eventually. It's too late anyway; she knows we're here, and she knows what we're coming for, too."

Liza did not at all like the way Mirabella pronounced the word *she*, as though it was something very large and very frightening.

Above them, the circling moribats gave a shrill

cry. The noise was terrible and made a dagger of ice-cold fear drive through Liza's center. The noise made her think of children abandoned in barren places without enough to eat; and open graves; and dark, bleak winter nights when through the thin air came the sounds of cars skidding and crashing on Route 47; and the squeak of a gurney's wheels on a hospital floor. It made her think of everything that was sad and lonely and depressing in the world.

Liza struggled to ignore the shrill wailing from above. She tried to remember the words to a song she and Patrick had made up years ago, for bath time, called "The Splish-Splosh Song," whose very first lyrics were "Drip and drop, slip and slop, watch the soap bubbles go pop, pop, pop." It was a stupid song, but it had always made Patrick giggle and so it usually made Liza feel better. She could not think of the tune, however. The moribats were too loud.

"I hate them," she burst out, and as if in response they fell silent and drifted away into the blackness. Instantly Liza felt better.

"You think *they're* bad," Mirabella said. "They're a nice piece of day-old sirloin on the very top of a trash heap compared to the scawgs! They're a fat wedge of only semi-moldy cheese! They're a one-worm apple!"

133

"Please," said Liza, who was starting to feel queasy. "I see your point."

Mirabella sniffed as though she doubted it.

"What are the scawgs?" Liza ventured, although she wasn't sure she wanted to know. Groups of moribats still massed up in the rocks around them, but at least these stayed silent, watching the travelers with their dull, milk-white eyes.

Mirabella shivered, and her tail twitched agitatedly. "Terrible creatures," she rasped hoarsely. "Ugly, ugly, ugly, inside and out. Originally part of the reptile family, of course, which explains it if you ask me. Evil, filthy things. Some say they're working for the queen. But the scawgs don't work for anyone but themselves. Always looking to fill their bellies."

"Yes, but what *are* they?" Liza demanded impatiently.

Mirabella's eyes darted back and forth, as though she feared they might be set upon by scawgs any second. "Hard to say, hard to say. They're crafty, nasty, crooked things—take different shapes at different times. But they can't hide their tails—oh no, never. Thick tails as long as snakes."

Liza's stomach flipped. She'd had quite enough of snakes for, well, ever.

"And the smell—they stink to high heaven! You

could bathe them in rose petals and they'd still smell worse than a barnyard in August. They eat the flesh of the dead; that's why the smell is so bad. It stays on their breath." Mirabella shook her head. "Very uncivilized. No manners at all."

Liza was horrified. "We won't—we won't run into any scawgs, will we?"

"Perhaps," Mirabella said, which wasn't very comforting. "It's hard to say." Then she sped up again, leaving Liza to imagine being picked to pieces by an oversize iguana with vicious dog-breath. She thought she would rather have been smashed into splinters by a tree snake.

By now even the bushes of hope had stopped growing. On either side of them were sheer chasms of rock, dark slated stone, and no plant life whatsoever. The few lumpen that still pulsed among the rocks did so weakly, faintly.

"Almost—there—" Mirabella panted out. "Just—a—little—farther—to—the—top—"

Then, from ahead, came sounds of singing.

The voice came from just beyond the final bend in the mountainous path, past two enormous, ancient rocks that leaned together to form a vaulted archway over the path. Whoever it was had the worst singing voice Liza had ever heard—worse even than that of her father, who couldn't even sing "Happy Birthday" in tune and had long ago given up trying.

They rounded a bend in the path, passed through the stone archway, and came suddenly to the end of the mountain. A small lip of rock jutted out over a sheer, vast, dizzying drop, an endless valley filled with floating mist.

A narrow wooden bridge stretched across the empty space, connecting the summit of their mountain to that of its twin, which Liza could make out very distantly, a looming dark shape beyond the mist. But the bridge did not seem particularly sturdy. Just looking at it made her feel nauseous.

"Are we—" She gulped. "Are we supposed to cross?"

"Not so fast!"

The voice came from a small pile of rubble. As Liza watched, the pile of rubble unfolded itself and stood, and Liza saw that it was *not* a pile of rubble after all, but an enormous mole, even larger and fatter than Mirabella, and dressed in gray robes so dingy and dusty and crinkly that Liza had mistaken the animal for stone. Its fur was the palest white, and its eyes—which were open, and twitching continuously back and forth—were clouded over, like a window completely covered in frost. The mole was blind, Liza realized.

"We come in peace," Mirabella said, and despite the fact that the mole surely couldn't appreciate it, she performed a low curtsy, so that her newspaper skirt touched the ground.

The mole's nose, also a perfect white, trembled wetly. "A human girl and a rat. What's your business on the other side?" The mole's voice was a raspy, hoarse whisper. He must have been the one singing, or attempting to; only a voice so terrible could mutilate a song so badly.

"We go to the nests," Mirabella said. "We have brought a gift for the queen of the spindlers."

Liza knew Mirabella only said it to help get them across, but she did not like the way the mole turned his milky, unblinking eyes toward her just then, and smiled, showing small, sharp teeth inside a glistening pink mouth.

"Ah yes. A gift." The way he said it was the way that a very hungry person might have said, *A sandwich*. "But nobody crosses the bridge without passing the test."

"What kind of test?" Liza asked warily.

"You must answer a riddle," the mole replied.

Liza's heart sank. Patrick had been given a book of riddles for his birthday last year, and she had never known the answer to a single one.

The mole cleared his throat loudly, and then began to rumble out, in a horrible approximation of song:

"What always runs but never walks,
Often murmurs but never talks,
Has a bed but never sleeps,
Has a mouth but never eats?"

"Oh dear." Mirabella took her tail in one paw and began to gnaw on it. "Oh dear, dear. How confounding. How confuddling! I've never been good with riddles, myself. Piddling things. Tricky, sticky, icky things."

"What always runs but never walks . . ." Liza repeated to herself.

The mole let out a cackling laugh. "Do you give up?"

"Give me a second, give me a second." Liza rubbed her forehead.

"Tick-tock, tick-tock!" the mole hummed, milky eyes roving endlessly. "Your time is running out."

"You didn't tell us there was a time limit!" Liza cried.

"Oh yes." The mole smiled, showing his slobbery pink tongue. "Hardly any time left to answer at all.

No one but the wise will journey 'cross the Bridge of Sighs."

"But that's not fair!" Liza burst out. This was exactly how things were Above: There were rules, but nobody told you about them, and you were somehow expected to know them anyway, and punished when you didn't.

"Fair?" The mole sniffed witheringly in her direction. "There is no such thing as fair. There is only the way things are."

This made Liza even madder. Suddenly she found she couldn't control her anger. She was sure that wasn't true. There was also the way things should be, and she knew it, and the mole knew it, and everybody Above and Below knew it, forever and always. Certain things were right, and certain things were not right. And she thought of Patrick, and she thought of her parents, and how they wouldn't listen, and the anger rose and crested inside her, and her heart let out a pulse of protest, and she continued, "It's not right, and you know it. We won't be turned back. We came all this way, and nearly got thrown into the dungeon by the nids and eaten by tree snakes and had to follow the river to—"

Liza shut her mouth quickly.

"Had to follow the river . . . ?" Mirabella prompted

her encouragingly, but for a moment Liza stayed perfectly still and silent, as the gears in her brain went *click-click-click* into place, and the meaning of the riddle became clear.

She looked up at the mole, her eyes shining. "The river," she said.

"We won't be turned back because of the river?" Mirabella repeated confusedly.

"No, no, no," Liza interrupted the rat excitedly. "I mean, that's the answer to the riddle. A river runs and doesn't walk, murmurs but doesn't talk, has a bed and never sleeps, and has a mouth but doesn't eat. That's right, isn't it?"

For a moment the mole let his disappointment show on his snout. Then he grunted, "You're much smarter than you smell."

Liza let out a whoop of satisfaction and chose not to worry too much about what stupidity smelled like.

"Well, that's that. Tip-top, and top shape, and topsy-turvy, and oopsy-daisy, off we go," Mirabella chanted. She adjusted her wig—which was again gravitating to the left—and started forward.

"Just a minute." The mole raised both paws and stepped in front of Mirabella, blocking her path. Despite his blindness, the animal was surprisingly quick on his feet. "I didn't say you could cross. You still have not paid the toll."

Liza gaped. "But you said—"

"I said you must pass the test," the mole said witheringly, showing his sharp teeth again. "But you must *also* pay the toll."

"We haven't got any money." Liza balled up her fists, feeling as though she would like to punch the mole directly in his ugly white snout. "We haven't got anything. My broom was snapped in two by a tree snake, and Mirabella lost her lunch box—"

"My purse," Mirabella corrected her primly.

"Her purse, and I'm only wearing one shoe . . ."

"Then I'm afraid you're out of luck," the mole said, folding his arms over his tunic and spreading his legs apart so that he was entirely blocking the entrance to the bridge.

Liza jammed her hands into her pockets. She still had Patrick's baseball, and the sock she had taken back from Mirabella, which was wrapped around her father's glasses. She offered all of it to the mole.

"This is everything we have," she said desperately. "Please—take it." Patrick would forgive her for losing his baseball again. He would have to. And her father would never know the difference.

The mole snorted disdainfully. "Trash!" he spat out. "I ask for a toll, and you insult me with this stinking mound of human trash! Get out of here, before I set the moribats on you both."

"Come on, Liza," Mirabella said quietly. "We won't find passage here."

Liza felt tears pushing at the back of her throat, burning just behind her eyes. As she stuffed the sock, glasses, and baseball back in her pocket, her fingers brushed against the seeds of hope.

"Wait!" Liza cried out. She reached into the pocket of her pajamas, and withdrew several seeds of hope. She had no idea whether this counted as a toll, but she offered them up to the mole anyway. "Hold out your paw," she said, and he did. His claws were dirt-encrusted and very sharp, and she was careful to avoid them as she counted three seeds into the very center of his paw.

Instantly the mole's whole snout loosened. A slow smile spread across his face as he stroked the seeds lovingly.

"Seeds of hope . . . ," he said quietly, milky eyes roaming aimlessly. "Ah, yes. I never thought . . ." Then he lapsed into silence, a look of utter content-ment on his face, as he continued to fondle the seeds carefully, shifting them from paw to paw.

Suddenly he seemed to remember that Liza and her companion were still there. He stepped abruptly out of the way, coughing.

"All right, then," he said. "Off you go."

Mirabella and Liza went forward onto the Bridge of Sighs, leaving the blind mole humming happily to himself, hunched over his seeds.

Chapter 14

THE GROANING TABLE

The bridge was made of very old wood that looked to Liza as though it would rot away at any second. It was very narrow, and they had to go single file—Mirabella, as always, taking up the lead. The bridge swayed dangerously beneath them, and Liza gripped tightly to the frayed rope handles.

She had been eager to cross, but once she was on the bridge she was filled with terror. The distant peak of the second Twin Mountain seemed miles and miles away, and on either side of them was a steep drop, a plummet of thousands of feet toward the River of

Knowledge. Now Liza understood why the bridge was called the Bridge of Sighs: The air was filled with ghostly echoes, as though thousands of phantoms were lamenting the travelers' progress.

"Don't like heights, never liked heights, don't like them," Mirabella chattered nervously.

"Just don't look down," Liza said, although she very much shared the rat's opinion, and did not feel nearly as confident as she wished to sound. The bridge gave another lurch, and she stifled a scream.

"Don't look down, don't look down, can't look down, got to look straight. Straight, wait, don't want to be late," Mirabella prattled on, semi-hysterical.

"Please." Liza was gripping the ropes so hard she could feel blisters developing on her palms. "Please, Mirabella. I am asking you, just this once. Please be quiet."

"Hush up, shush up," Mirabella chanted quietly.

At last they were within sight of the solid slate side of the second of the two twin peaks. Liza was tempted to break into a run, but she feared that any quick motions would cause the rotting wood to fall away under their feet. And so they made slow, shuffling progress along the bridge. Liza's heart hammered painfully against her ribs, and her palms burned where the rope slid across her skin.

Just fifteen more feet . . . Liza told herself. *Just twelve more feet.* She imagined Patrick standing on the opposite side of the bridge. She focused on his face, held it in her mind, fixated on the three freckles at the tip of his nose, which in summertime merged and multiplied.

The bridge swayed beneath her; the wind sighed and heaved.

And then, underneath the wind, Liza detected another sound. At first she was sure she must be imagining it, and she paused for a moment, straining to hear.

Laughter floated to them through the mist. Someone—a few someones—were laughing in the darkness, among the swirling mists. Laughter rolled and echoed off the jagged rocks. Liza thought she heard bells, too, and a distant drumming, and she was instantly reminded of the time several years earlier when her parents had had their Christmas Eve party, and she had woken up in the middle of the night to the sound of muffled laughter, and crept quietly to the stairs, and seen her mother asleep on the couch, eyes closed, and a few people still in the living room, dancing in bare feet, while her father played the guitar. It was the strangest moment of her life, and had filled her with both amazement and terror.

She had not even known that her father knew how to play.

This moment was just like that: Coming across music in such a barren, forbidding place made her feel both awe and fear.

She was so focused on the strange sounds she did not even notice that her feet were no longer on the swaying, tilting bridge; they had crossed over safely.

"Well," Mirabella said, adjusting her wig. "Well, well. That was interesting. I'm not sure—oh, I'm hardly certain at all—that I like bridges. Nasty things. Swishing and swaying—sashaying!"

"Shhh," Liza hushed her again. "I'm trying to listen."

Mirabella muttered something under her breath about Below being a "free place of speech," but Liza ignored her. There was a new quality to the air, a smokiness, and at first she could hardly believe it.

"Do you smell . . ." She inhaled deeply and her stomach growled. "Is it possible that . . . I think I'm smelling . . ."

Mirabella's eyes suddenly widened, and a spark appeared in their center. "Meat!" the rat cried out. "Meat! Meat to eat!" And she dropped on all fours and began to scamper down the path.

"Wait for me!" Liza called after her. She ran as

fast as she could, sending a shower of loose stones hurtling over the edge of the mountain and down toward the river below.

But Liza could not slow down. She had never, ever, ever in her whole life been so hungry: She realized that now. With every stumbling step, the smell of grilling meat grew stronger, and there were other delicious smells that hovered alongside it: hot pancakes and thick maple syrup, steaming bowls of chicken noodle soup, baked macaroni and cheese with buttered bread crumbs, golden french fries, chocolate-chip cookies straight from the oven, oozing butter.

The path turned a corner and opened into a broad, flat clearing, as though a chunk of the mountain had been lifted cleanly away, leaving a flat-bottomed bowl. At its center was a long wooden table piled high with every delicious food Liza could think of, and some she couldn't: roasted turkeys with skins the brown of mahogany; vivid purple grapes that glistened in the cheerful glow of the torches, which had been set all along the periphery of the clearing and filled it with a festive, flickering light.

Four women were sitting at the table, laughing: one with brown hair, one with hair the russet red of an apple, one with jet-black tresses, and one with a braid that was the soft blond of early sunshine. All of them had the same pretty, round faces and large blue eyes, and Liza decided right away that they must be sisters.

They were laughing and singing. The black-haired woman had a tambourine in her pale white hands and was beating out a jangly rhythm while the red-haired woman strummed a tiny guitar. There were red flowers, with bulbs as large as Liza's head, placed all around the table, letting off their own delicious scent—like honey and pine needles and a fresh ocean breeze, all at once. They seemed almost to nod in time to the music.

"Look, sisters," the red-haired one said, glancing up from the table. "We have visitors."

The black-haired one laid down her tambourine. All four women turned to stare, and Liza felt her cheeks burning, and swallowed several times. Her mouth was watering, and it was all she could do not to rush to the table and start cramming her cheeks with all the food she could, like a chipmunk.

"H-hello," Liza said shyly.

"Hello," the women chorused together. They were so beautiful they were almost frightening, despite their warm smiles.

Mirabella stood in anxious silence, fidgeting with her skirt and shawl and wig, until Liza reached out and elbowed her sharply in her furry side. Mirabella jumped and landed in a deep curtsy, stuttering out, "Charmed, charmed. Very indebted."

"Don't be shy," said the blond one. "Please—come and sit with us."

"You must be hungry," said the red-haired one, whose smile was the biggest of them all. "Very hungry."

"Um—yes. As a matter of fact, we are." As if to prove it, Liza's stomach gave a tremendous gurgle.

"Please," said the brown-haired one. "Eat with us. My sister was just about to play a song."

"I'll play," the red-haired one said. Her teeth were large and square and white. "And you eat."

"Eat, eat," the other three murmured.

"Thank you." Liza could have sobbed in gratitude. She nearly broke into a run crossing the clearing, and she could sense that Mirabella was also having trouble controlling herself. She wanted so badly to sit down, and tear at a turkey leg with her hands, and eat and eat, until she could barely stand.

Mirabella sat down next to the blond woman.

"What a lovely skirt," the blond woman said, and she reached out and caressed Mirabella's ears. "And what nice, soft fur you have."

Liza had never known that rats could blush, but

Mirabella did then. She turned a dark crimson, and even her whiskers took on a reddish hue.

"Thank you," the rat muttered and then, deeply embarrassed, picked up a whole wedge of blue cheese and stuffed it unceremoniously into her cheeks so that no one would expect her to speak again.

Liza took a seat next to the red-haired woman, who had started strumming again softly. The music was lovely and reminded Liza of sunshine and endless laughter. She picked up a soft, warm roll and sank her teeth into its crust, and almost cried out with joy when butter dribbled down her cheek.

"You must have traveled very far," said the black-haired sister.

"Mm-hmm," Liza mumbled, with her mouth full of apple pie and sweet maple syrup. "Vewy faw." She was too hungry to be embarrassed about talking with her mouth full.

"Where have you come from?" asked the blond one, as she helped Liza pile her plate with biscuits, bacon, and sticky toffee.

"From Abuff," Liza said, as she swallowed a biscuit practically whole, washing it down with a swig of chocolate milk from the stone mug the red-haired sister placed in front of her.

Strangely, the more she ate, the more a pit seemed

to open inside of her: pain, agony, a terrible, shredding hunger.

She could tell that Mirabella felt the same way. The rat had forgotten all her manners. She was perched on her hind legs on the bench, bent over the enormous turkey, working away with her two sharp teeth, clawing frantically at its flesh. Bits of browned skin dangled from the rat's fingernails. Liza began to feel nauseous, though it did nothing to quell the hunger.

"Eat, eat," the sisters chanted softly, encouragingly. The music continued to play: The tambourine beat out a soft rhythm, and the notes of the guitar seemed to wrap Liza's mind in a soft, enveloping cloud, making other thoughts difficult. She could feel the music, stretching inside her, like long, soft fingers; the perfume of the food and the flowers made her feel very sleepy. She and the rat had been on their way somewhere, she was sure of it. . . . There was something she was supposed to do . . . someone she was looking for . . .

She frowned. The memory was just out of reach, an irritating twinge among all that soft loveliness of the music. It would be better, far better, to stay here and eat, to put all other ideas out of her mind. She would eat and eat; she could eat forever here, and never be full.

She reached for a piece of fried chicken and tore at a leg with her teeth. Surprisingly, the chicken and the toffee tasted quite good together. She would have to remember to tell Patrick.

Patrick. The name sent a much-needed jolt through Liza's body. Of course! She was on her way to find the spindlers. She was on her way to rescue Patrick.

Wait, Liza tried to say, but the word wouldn't rise up from the thick fog in her brain. She reached out to pour herself a glass of water and was surprised to see that her arm seemed to be wobbly, like a mirage on the horizon fading in and out. Her eyes felt heavy. She felt her arm drop to her side.

"Sleep, sleep," the sisters chanted.

No, Liza tried to say.

Across from her, Mirabella was asleep, drooling, snout-down in a pile of creamy mashed potatoes. Liza fought the fog, and the sensation of heaviness all through her. She fought her way out of the music; it was like swimming upward through a thick, murky pond. She gathered her strength and pushed forcefully away from the table, stumbling to her feet. In the process she knocked over one of the enormous flowers around the table.

A horrible, piercing whine filled the air, and to Liza's horror, the flower began to writhe and thrash, as though in pain. All the sisters were shouting now, and Liza saw that when angry they were not beautiful at all; their faces appeared to be melting. They were growing old in front of her; their skin was lined and gray, almost rotten-looking.

Terror carved a little clear space in Liza's mind. "What's happening? What are they?" she cried.

"Come here, you disgusting little worm." The black-haired sister stood, lunging for her, and in that moment Liza's blood froze, and she saw that the woman was not a woman at all, but some other thing. The bottom half of her body was covered in thick, green-and-black scales, and she had an enormous tail that tapered to a razor-sharp point. And as the thing—the ugly, terrible thing—revealed itself fully, Liza was hit with a terrible, choking smell, an overwhelming stench that made her gag reflexively.

Everything was confusion; broken images. Liza's body was still clumsy, heavy. She couldn't move. She couldn't think. The red-haired one was screaming and shrieking, mouth wide open to reveal an awful coal-black tongue, clapping her hands with glee. The brown-haired monster had sprung onto the table—landing directly in a bowl of chocolate pudding and shattering it—and, with tail lashing, was binding the still-sleeping Mirabella's paws with heavy rope.

Liza tried to run. She got no more than a few steps before the red-haired thing intercepted her, catching her by the shoulders.

"Not so fast, dearie," the thing hissed.

Liza fought the urge to gag. The smell brought tears to her eyes.

"Let me go!" she screamed, flailing. But the monster was strong, and easily wrestled her down to the ground. Liza was brought cheek-first against the hard stone; her arms were wrenched behind her painfully, and she felt thick cords of rope digging into the skin of her wrists.

A word rose up through the fog in Liza's brain, as though her nocturna was speaking to her from very far away.

Scawgs, the voice said.

Then a curtain came down over Liza's mind, and all was blackness.

Chapter 15

THE RIVER OF KNOWLEDGE

When Liza woke, her first impression was that she was at home, in her bed, and had somehow gotten squished up against one of her stuffed animals. Perhaps she had accidentally rolled toward the wall, as she sometimes did, and had her face buried in Mr. Ted, the stuffed bear she had had since she was very young. . . .

Except that Mr. Ted was very dirty, and smelled of cheese. . . . And her bed was very bumpy, and lumpy, and hard.

Then she snapped into awareness and realized that

she was in the back of a wooden cart no bigger than a wheelbarrow, sandwiched next to Mirabella; and in her sleep she had rolled over and was pressed face-first into the rat's fur. She rolled onto her back, sputtering and coughing out the disgusting rat taste, and wondered whether her mother would make her go to the doctor for a special round of shots, and if so, whether Patrick would be impressed by how calmly she could bear the needles.

That is, if she ever saw Patrick again. Or her mother, for that matter.

At this point, Liza wouldn't have minded going to the doctor every single day for the rest of her life, and getting multiple shots, if only she could be safely Above again.

They were being bumped down the mountainside by the scawg with the yellow hair: hair, Liza now saw, that was dirty and full of insects. Ahead of them, the other scawgs were prancing merrily down the steep path. One of the scawgs was dancing; the other two were still playing the guitar and the tambourine, although now the music was horrible, loud and clashing like car horns and brakes squealing and fingers on chalkboards, all at once.

Mirabella was just waking up. The rat yawned and opened her eyes.

"Oh dear. Dear, dear, dear. I must have dozed for a minute or two," she said.

"You didn't doze," Liza whispered. "You were drugged, and we've been captured by scawgs."

"Scawgs?" Mirabella's eyes widened in alarm. "Where?"

"See for yourself." Liza indicated to their captors with her chin.

Mirabella let out a squeak of fear and tried to sit up. Then, realizing her paws were tied, she started thrashing, and in the process elbowed Liza in the stomach.

"Stop writhing," Liza said. "You're bumping me."

"Oh, this is bad. Very, very bad."

"Will you be quiet? I'm trying to think." The rat's grating voice, in combination with a loud, rushing sound that filled the air around them—Liza could not tell where it came from—made her head hurt. Her brain was still a bit fuzzy, and the noise wasn't helping.

The cart came jerkily and suddenly to a stop. When Liza managed to wriggle into a seated position, she saw that the rushing sound came from the river; they had worked their way all the way down the other side of the Twin Mountains and were at the very edge of the water. Here the river was enormously wide, and a very dark purple. There was a flat wooden boat sitting on its rocky banks. Liza saw immediately that the scawgs were intending to float them down the river.

"Up and at 'em, my pretties." This was the black-haired scawg, who loomed over them, grinning, with filthy and rotten teeth. Liza held her breath against the stench. "Ready for a little boat ride?"

She heaved Liza easily over one shoulder, and Mirabella over the other, as though neither weighed anything at all, and carried them down to the boat, where she dropped them roughly. Once again Liza found herself with a mouth full of rat fur.

She pulled away, making a face. "Do you ever bathe, Mirabella?"

Mirabella appeared offended. "Twice a week, regular as pie. In the sewers next to the water treatment plant."

Perhaps, Liza thought, when this was all over she would have her mother make an appointment at the dentist's; for the first time in her life, she thought she wouldn't mind having her teeth scrubbed.

Three of the scawgs joined them in the boat, two of them still playing their terrible music and shrieking merrily. The fourth pushed them off into the river and then sprang into the boat herself, with surprising agility for such a huge, ugly creature. Liza noticed that all four scawgs were very careful to avoid touching the water. The black-haired scawg stood at the prow of the long boat, using a twisted black pole to push away from the banks.

As they moved toward the center of the river, they were caught up in a swift current. Even though the black-haired scawg did not need to punt anymore with the pole, she remained standing at the front of the boat, wind whipping her filthy mane behind her, cackling happily, like a child at the front of a roller coaster. The scawgs' merriment made Liza deeply uneasy. Anything pleasant to the scawgs must surely be very, very unpleasant for her and Mirabella.

"Mirabella," Liza whispered. "Did you mean what you said earlier? About the river being deadly for all but the nocturni?"

"Oh, the river," Mirabella moaned as the boat rocked in the water. She was nearly in agony; Liza hoped the rat would not get seasick. The last thing she needed was to be coated in rodent vomit. "The river is *very* deadly. *Very* dangerous. Oh yes. Stay away from the river. Stay away from—eek!" The boat lurched, and tears sprang up in Mirabella's eyes. Liza could tell she was too frightened to be useful.

"Where are you taking us?" she called out to the scawgs, over the clamorous noise of their music.

"Wouldn't you like to know?" said the blond-haired

one, sticking out a mottled green tongue in Liza's direction.

Liza pretended to be unimpressed. "I bet you don't even know," she said, feigning a yawn. "I bet you're lost."

"Lost!" the red-haired one scoffed. "Impossible. We know every twist and tunneled turn between the Twin Mountains and the Black Pit."

The Black Pit: So that was where they were headed. Liza did not like the sound of it.

"What are you planning to do with us?" she demanded, trying to keep the quiver from her voice.

The scawgs began to chuckle humorlessly. The red-haired scawg continued strumming on her guitar, picking at the strings with her blackened fingernails. "Oh dear. What a terribly difficult question. It's so hard to say, isn't it, sisters?"

"Very hard."

"So many choices!"

"So many *recipes*."

"We could boil you, of course." She grinned, and Liza saw a hungry white light burning in her eyes. "Or bake you, baste you, stuff you, and roll you. Fry you in oil—"

"But grilling is a healthier alternative," the blond one put in, pouting. "And you know I'm on a diet."

"We could cream you, steam you, and stuff you in a pie!"

Liza shivered.

"You feasted at our table," the brown-haired one said, running her tongue over her teeth. "So, you see, it's only fair. Now you must be the feast."

"That's not fair at all!" Liza cried out above the scawgs' cackling laughter, though she knew it would do no good.

The boat continued to speed down the river, rocking slightly, and Mirabella continued to moan, and the scawgs continued to laugh and play their music, and Liza thought furiously. She would not be boiled or stuffed—or even grilled. It was, in fact, out of the question.

She remembered, suddenly, the time that she and Patrick had been playing cop and criminal and she had been the criminal, and he had tied her up with an old jump rope in the backyard. But then instead of releasing her as he was supposed to, he had gotten bored and wandered back into the house to play a video game (and, as she later discovered, eat the very last of the Froot Loops).

And Liza had screamed at the top of her lungs, but it was not until almost two hours later that her mother had returned from grocery shopping and heard her. And Patrick had been punished, and Liza smothered in kisses and given ice cream before and after dinner, and so it had not ended badly at all.

But no one would come to the rescue here, no matter how long and loud Liza screamed.

No. She would have to escape the scawgs herself.

Liza groped along the bottom of the boat. It was a very old boat, and uncomfortable to lie on: The wood was warped and full of splinters. Liza despised splinters. One time, in the tree house, she had gotten her new soft sweater—the one in the perfect cream color, which she had had to beg and beg for—caught on a splinter and it had ripped a hole . . .

It had ripped a hole . . .

Straight through the fabric!

That was it!

Liza felt with her fingers until she located a particularly large and nasty splinter of wood, which was digging mercilessly into her lower back. She squirmed and wriggled until the rope binding her wrists was positioned just above its jagged edges; then she sawed her wrists back and forth and prayed. After only a minute, she began to feel a gradual loosening around her wrists. A feeling of joy swelled inside her. It was working.

"Oh dear, oh dear," Mirabella groaned, keeping

her eyes squeezed tightly shut, as the boat continued whipping downriver. "All that rocking. Terrible. I think I'll be sick."

"Don't even think about it," Liza whispered. "Now hush. I'm trying to concentrate."

Back and forth, back and forth: The tension around her wrists let up a little more, and then a little more, and then—*snap!*—she was free. Liza contained a cry of excitement. She was far from safe.

"Mirabella." She leaned over and pressed her mouth directly against the rat's fuzzy ear. "I've managed to get my hands free."

"You what?" Mirabella's eyes flew open.

"Shh." Liza reached over and clamped a hand over the rat's snout. Fortunately the Scawgs were engrossed in a heated argument about whether human went better with buttered potatoes or roasted squash, and were paying no attention to their captives. "We must be very quiet and very careful. I'm going to untie you, okay?"

Mirabella nodded, eyes wide.

Liza helped the rat roll over onto her side, so that her paws, and the rope tied tightly around them, were visible; then Liza began working slowly and carefully at the knots, keeping one eye on the scawgs at the front of the boat. The work was made even more difficult because the boat kept tipping and dipping, and sending Mirabella rolling back into Liza, squeaking with fear, so that it seemed she almost *wanted* the scawgs to hear her. And as soon as Liza did get Mirabella onto her side again, the rat's tail—released from underneath her—would begin whipping excitedly in Liza's face.

"For goodness' sake," Liza said, "can't you control that thing?"

"I can't help it," Mirabella whispered back miserably. "Nervous habit."

But at last Liza was successful, and when the ropes came off Mirabella's paws, Liza once again leaned in to whisper to her. Her stomach was full of a thick, coiled fear; she was not looking forward to this bit, not at all.

"Mirabella," she said. "We must swim for it."

Mirabella looked even more frightened than when she had first woken up in the boat with the scawgs. She grabbed Liza's shirt frantically. "We can't! Oh no! That is a very, very bad idea."

"We have no choice," Liza insisted. And she knew it was true. "I am not going to be baked into a pie and eaten."

Mirabella looked as though she thought that might be preferable. "But the river . . ."

"You've warned me about the river. But it's our only hope. I, for one, am going to swim for it."

Liza sucked in a deep breath and sat up. At that moment a few things happened in very rapid succession:

One of the flowers began lashing its long stem crazily back and forth, whipping Liza in the face and sending her tumbling onto her back.

The scawgs, seeing the commotion, began to scream, and two of them rushed toward Liza and Mirabella.

The boat tipped dangerously to one side, and Liza rolled toward its edge.

Mirabella shouted, "I won't let you!" and made a dive for Liza, managing to get a claw around the second of Liza's sneakers.

The boat tipped;

The flower twisted;

Liza's foot came free of the sneaker;

And Liza went tumbling, suddenly, into the roaring, rushing River of Knowledge.

Chapter 16

Liza

THE REWARD

Everything was noise and confusion—so much noise it made Liza feel as though her head was about to explode.

Liza fought desperately to reach the surface of the river, but she was so confused and terrified she did not know which way was up or down. This was unlike any water she had ever known. The river was full of swirling images, mixed together, jumbled up: dark stone that flowed like a river across the surface of a pale blue planet; a single drop of dew trembling at the edge of an enormous purple petal; stars racing across a pink sky; a child running through a luscious green field.

But there were terrible things too: faces that leered at her; galloping, snorting horses that reared above her and brought their enormous hooves driving toward her face; green creatures, covered in dark green algae, that grabbed at her ankles and tugged her downward.

Her chest was collapsing. She couldn't breathe. Her mouth was full of choking red dust: a tornado, in the center of the river, spiraling toward her. A baby was crying. A woman and a man, both wearing starched white gloves, danced in a room made entirely of gold, while an orchestra played. Then a bull, snorting, massive; she could feel its heat, she would be trampled, she would die.

More nightmare creatures, with mouths looped around with seaweed, like some horrible stitching, and long fingers, rotting.

Liza, Liza, Liza, they chanted, in voices that were as soft as a snake's hiss. *Come join us, Liza. Live forever, Liza. Play forever, Liza.*

No, she tried to scream; but the weight of the water was everywhere: the noise, the heat, the horrible faces and places and things. And the last of her air went; the pain in her lungs was huge. She swallowed, gulping a choking sand, a choking dust, choking—

She was choking—

Then suddenly, just like that, the creatures let go, and Liza was lifted; she broke the surface of the river and gulped in air, sobbing and grateful, as the swift currents released her. Mirabella, sopping wet, heaved her out of the water and onto the rocky banks. Liza was shivering and sobbing, coughing up water. Mirabella had lost her wig, her shawl, and the last of her skirt. The rat stood, skinny, naked, trembling.

The scawgs were nowhere to be seen.

"What did I tell you?" Mirabella cried shrilly, but before she could get any further, Liza had thrown her arms around the rat's shoulders.

"Oh, Mirabella!" she cried, clinging tightly to the shivering rat. "Thank you, thank you, thank you!"

Mirabella's body went rigid: Remember that she had never, not once in her whole life, been hugged.

Liza's teeth were chattering, though not from the cold. Her mind was still clouded with the river's roiling visions; she was sure she would have died had she been submerged any longer.

"You saved my life." Liza was too grateful to care about the taste of wet rat fur in her mouth.

"You are the bravest, truest rat I've ever known. No. You are the bravest, truest *friend* I've ever had."

A tiny spasm passed through Mirabella's body, but Liza didn't notice.

She didn't notice, either, the clicking sounds from all around them, the *tic-tic-tic* of tiny nails against the rocks.

She pulled away from Mirabella but kept her hands on the rat's bony shoulders, stooping just a little so she could stare the rat directly in her eyes. "And I want you to know, Mirabella, that you are beautiful. You are beautiful just like this, as you are, with no makeup or clothes or anything."

Liza was not just saying this to be nice. The rat did appear beautiful to her just then, with her large black eyes and long silken whiskers, and curled gray fur, still dripping water.

Mirabella gave a short cry, almost of pain, and to Liza's surprise, tears sprang up in the rat's eyes.

Believing the rat must be overwhelmed, Liza moved once again to hug her.

"That's okay," she said kindly. "You don't have to say anything."

Mirabella gave another mangled cry. "It's not okay!" She broke free of Liza's arms. "Oh, Miss Liza. I'm sorry. I'm so, so sorry."

"Sorry?" Liza laughed. "What do you have to be sorry . . ." But the laughter, and the words, dried up in Liza's throat.

By then she had heard it: the unmistakable *tic-tic-tic* of the nails. Fear seized her, and her body went all at once to ice. She did not consciously think of turning around, but then she found herself turning; everything seemed to happen in slow motion.

"Well, well, well." The voice behind her was no louder than a whisper, like the rustle of dry leaves in autumn. "We've been expecting you for quite some time now."

Liza's heart stopped: spindlers, dozens and dozens of them, crowded black shapes massed along the rocks, watched her amusedly with their crescent eyes. The spindler that had spoken was the size of a large house cat and covered all over in prickly black hair. Even its hands were covered in hair. Its fingernails were long, sharp, and painted red.

"You have my brother," Liza managed to croak out.

"Perhaps," the spindler said. It had a wide mouth, and two long, curved pincers that made it seem as though it was constantly grinning. The spindler turned toward Mirabella. "You've done your job well, rat. Admirably well. The queen will be pleased. She will be sure to remember your services to us after we have

171

feasted, when all the world Below is ours."

Next to Liza, Mirabella was miserably chewing her tail. Liza felt a blackness rise inside her, a wave of cold fury.

"You—you're on *their* side?" She was shaking so badly she had to ball her hands against her thighs.

Mirabella let out a pathetic and hapless squeak, which was as good as a full confession of guilt.

"And all this time you pretended to be helping me, and really you were just leading me here to—to be *trapped*?"

The spindler let out a hollow laugh, and the other spindlers joined in, so the air was full of a low rustling: It made Liza think of rain pounding against black winter branches. "You didn't really think the rat offered to help out of the goodness of her heart, did you?" Contempt was obvious in the spindler's tone. "Don't they teach you *anything* Above?"

"I trusted you," Liza said in a bare whisper. Mirabella groaned and clamped her hands over her ears.

"Everyone knows you can't trust a rat." The spindler gestured for one of its many companions to come forward. "Give the slimy creature its reward."

One of the other spindlers scuttled forward. In its two front hands it held a small mirrored compact made of cheap plastic, like the kind Liza's aunt Virginia got at department stores when she spent more than twenty-five dollars on face creams and perfume.

This was too much.

"A *mirror*?" Liza felt the heat rushing back; she found herself wishing, cruelly, that she still had her broom. Now she would gladly bop Mirabella over the head. "You traded me for a cheap plastic mirror?"

Mirabella still had her paws over her ears and was shaking her head back and forth. "Bad, bad, bad, bad, bad rat," she muttered. "Can't trust a dirty, filthy rat. No good for anything."

Liza took a step forward, and Mirabella squeaked with fear. She brought her paws defensively in front of her chest, as though worried Liza was going to attack her. But Liza could only say, "I wanted to be your *friend*. I thought we *were* friends. Do you understand that?"

Mirabella froze. Her mouth fell open, but no words or sounds emerged.

"All right, rat," the spindler said, with unconcealed contempt. "You've done your job. Take your trinket, and be off with you. Unless you, too, would like to stay for the Feasts . . . ?"

Again the titter went up from the other spindlers.

Mirabella took up the mirror, squeezing it tightly in both paws. But she kept her eyes on Liza, and her whiskers quivered. She closed her mouth and opened it again. Still nothing.

Liza felt herself seized on all sides by tiny, clammy hands, as the spindlers crowded around her. But she was too sad to care; she couldn't think of anything but Mirabella's betrayal. Now she really was all alone in the underworld. She had absolutely no one to help her.

"To the queen," rasped the largest spindler.

Liza allowed herself to be pushed forward by the seething mass of spider-people. At the last second, she turned around. Mirabella was still standing, frozen, by the edge of the River of Knowledge, clutching her mirror.

"I would have given you all the mirrors you wanted," Liza said sadly.

"Miss Liza—" Mirabella started to say, but Liza did not hear the rest of her words. The pressure of all those tiny, terrible hands turned her left, around a bend in the road, and the rat disappeared from view.

Chapter 17

THE QUEEN OF THE SPINDLERS

These were the nests, the home of the spindlers, and the heart of the world Below. Every rock was covered in quivering gray spiderwebs, and among them thousands of spindlers of all different sizes—some as small as regular spiders, some as large as poodles—watched Liza with their unblinking green eyes, and clicked their nails against the rocks, and made hooting sounds of glee as she passed.

Above her, a series of webs was strung like a canopy. Spindlers scurried above her head, taunting her, and try as she did to appear courageous, she could not stop herself from shaking. She imaged spindlers dropping on her from above, snaking their nails down her back.

Beyond the webs, the moribats were circling and calling to one another shrilly; and next to her something enormous—it must have been the size of a golf cart—scuttled along the rocks, and the air was full of shadows. Liza gave up on being brave and allowed herself to feel afraid.

After a short while they came to a place where the rocks had, over time, been chiseled away by the digging, scratching motion of hundreds of thousands of sharp nails: It was an enormous cavern, covered so completely with webs it looked as though a powdery gray snow had fallen. Columns of rock rose up from the cavern floor; between them were slung more silvery threads, on which masses of moribats were swinging, and preening their featherless bodies, and watching everything with milky white eyes.

The spindlers all around Liza dispersed, scattering into the dark corners of the cavern: all except the largest one, who remained next to Liza, keeping one of its six hands firmly planted on her back.

"We have brought the girl, my queen," it called out into the murky darkness in front of them.

"Very good," came the horrible, grating reply. To Liza it sounded like a body being dragged slowly over gravel.

Then the darkness in front of them began to move, and take shape; eight legs, each the size of tree trunks, unfolded, and the thing shook itself, and stood. Liza found herself trembling in its enormous shadow: So this was the queen.

Liza had vastly underestimated the queen's size. She was as large as a house—a small house, but a house nonetheless. Her jointed and hair-covered limbs tapered to hands that seemed horribly out of place; they were the hands of a beauty, with long, thin fingers and sharp, curved nails, painted a swirling opal color. Her eyes were a glittering purple, dark crescents set like stones above her sprawling mouth, and her glistening, venom-tipped fangs.

Even the spindler that had escorted Liza thus far seemed terrified. When the queen, with a flick of one of her eight wrists, gestured dismissively for it to leave, the spindler scuttled gratefully off into a corner. Liza was left alone.

"So"—the queen loomed over Liza—"you have come to see the nests."

"I have come to rescue my brother's soul," Liza said, wishing that her voice would not shake so badly.

"Ah, your brother." The queen smiled—if the monstrous pulling apart of its mouth could be called a smile—and gave another dismissive flick of her wrist. "The world is full of brothers and sisters, mothers, fathers, friends. Everyone means something to someone else. It is extremely tiresome to keep track of. The rat brought you here?"

Thinking of Mirabella made Liza's anger flare again. "The rat tricked me," she said. "I thought she was trying to help. I thought she was a friend."

"A rat is a rat, and will always be a rat, and nothing but. Haven't you learned anything yet, my dear? We are never anything but what we were born to be." As the queen of the spindlers spoke, she seemed to shrink: smaller and smaller and smaller, until she was no larger than a kitten. And then, just like that, she sprang. Instinctively Liza ducked. But the queen had missed her, landing soundlessly on one of the pillars just to Liza's left; then she zigzagged to a pillar on Liza's right, leaving a thin, glistening strand of silver thread between them. Liza saw that she was weaving.

"You see?" the queen said, as she slid and skated through the air, leaving silver threads as she went. "I may be the queen of the spindlers—the most powerful creature Below—but in the end I must do what I was born to do. I must make webs."

Liza watched, amazed. The queen moved rapidly, a dark blur: and in no time at all an enormous web had taken shape in front of Liza's eyes, full of loops and twists and patterns that reminded her of the most delicate lace. It would have been beautiful if it were not for the queen, who settled in the middle of the web, watching Liza with her intelligent eyes. Liza was not comforted by the queen's smallness; somehow she was even more terrifying this way. She seemed quicker now, more likely to attack.

"Give me my brother back." Liza forced the words out past the fear.

The queen smiled, displaying a set of glistening fangs. "Ah, that I won't do. We need him, you know. We need all of them. I fear my friends are getting very hungry."

A deep chill went through Liza's body, as the spindlers massed in the dark recesses of the cavern tittered and rustled, and clicked their fangs together, as though they were already preparing to feast.

Liza took refuge in one of her favorite phrases. "It's not fair," she said. "Patrick's soul doesn't belong to you. You have to give it back."

"Fair?" The queen swayed a little in the middle of her shimmering web, seemingly amused. "My dear, misguided child. Nothing could be more fair. Possession is in ownership, after all, and victory is in the spoils. I wanted Patrick's soul, so I took it, and because I took it, it belongs to me."

Liza was growing more muddled by the second. "But it's not right," she insisted.

"Right, wrong," the queen scoffed. "Haven't you learned that there is no such thing? There is only what you are prepared to take, and what you are prepared to give."

"Fine. Then I'll just take his soul back," Liza said with more confidence than she felt.

"Ah, now we're getting somewhere." The queen of the spindlers descended a little farther on the web, gripping the threads with her long fingers, so that she and Liza were at eye level. "You are talking about a kind of contest?"

"I—I guess so," Liza stammered.

"A test of wills. I, of course, have always liked tests, hurdles, riddles, puzzles, traps, and snares." As if to prove this, at that moment a moribat—weaving carelessly through the cavern—collided with the queen's web. Instantly it became entangled. The more it fluttered, the more it became hopelessly entwined in the threads of the web, until the queen reached out, snatched it up in two of her hands, and dropped the struggling creature into her mouth.

"What was I saying?" the queen mumbled through a mouthful of moribat. A small white bone slipped from the queen's mouth and clattered to the ground, and Liza had to turn away to keep from being sick.

"You want your brother's soul. I do not want to part with it. But if you manage to take it from me . . . well, then, I suppose it belongs to you. Doesn't that seem fair?"

"I guess so," Liza said, unconvinced. She felt as though the queen was weaving webs inside her brain, making everything complex and confused.

"Good, good." The queen, having swallowed the last of the moribat, licked her fingers in a satisfied way. "Then how about a few small tests? If you pass, you can have your brother back. If you fail, I get to keep his soul."

Around her, the other spindlers scuttled closer, watching and judging her response. Crescent eyes winked at her from the dark.

Liza's heart was beating very fast. "What do I have to do?"

"The Web of Souls lies at the end of the corridor. To get to it, you must pass through three rooms." She gestured to a vaulted space in the rocks at the end of the cavern: the entrance to the first room, presumably.

"If you can get to your brother, you can have him."

"That's it?" Liza asked. It sounded too easy; she was sure that the queen had some other trick up one hairy arm. "You swear?"

"Word of honor." The queen raised a slender hand, grinning. Around her came tittering sounds: The other spindlers were laughing. *Tic-tic-tic* went their nails on the stone, as they inched closer, waiting for Liza's reaction, waiting to see what she would do.

Liza felt fear needling in her stomach. *Wrong,* a voice said inside her. She knew the queen could not be trusted.

On the other hand, she had no choice.

"All right," Liza said at last. "I'll go."

"Excellent," the queen said. She dropped lightly from her web to the ground. Then, perceiving the fallen bone of the moribat, she scooped it up quickly and chomped it down greedily. Liza could not prevent herself from shivering.

"This way, dearie," the queen said. Liza followed her, ducking under the enormous web that now filled half the cavern, careful to avoid its silken strands. She imagined herself caught, like the moribat, struggling in the threads.

The other spindlers came out of the darkness and followed Liza and the queen at a safe distance. She could feel them, all around her, a slow compression: It felt like someone had reached out and put a hand in her stomach and squeezed. She was afraid.

At the end of the cavern was a long tunnel of darkness; at the far end, a plain wooden door was set in the stone. Liza's mouth felt very dry.

It's just dark, she thought. *That's the only reason I'm so afraid. There is nothing else to be scared of.* She wished she had a lumer-lumpen with her now.

Then she thought, *Being afraid of the dark is for babies.* She thought of Patrick curled up next to her in the night, as they made a game of finding shadow-shapes on the walls, and felt slightly better.

"Whenever you're ready," the queen said, with a flourish of a hand. Despite the politeness of her tone, her eyes glowed unpleasantly.

Liza took one shuffling step forward into the dark, and then another. She kept her eyes fixed on the wooden door ahead of her. One more step, and then another. The air was damp, warm, and close; she almost couldn't breathe. Too quickly she had reached the door, and she lifted one hand to its rusted brass handle.

"Oh, one more thing I forgot to mention."

Liza whipped around at the sound of the queen's voice. The queen had swelled again, just a little, so she now almost entirely blocked the entrance to the dark corridor. Her eyes glowed brighter and brighter; they had gone from purple to a bright bloodred. Around her and between her legs, the other spindlers were pressing close; fangs dripping, they watched Liza's progress closely.

"If you fail to reach your brother," the queen said, "it will not just be his soul that belongs to us."

More laughter from the spindlers. And now Liza felt the weight of something else all around her: It was their hunger, their slurping, endless hunger. She could feel it pulling at her like an underwater current from all sides.

"It will be your soul too," the queen said, as the spindlers' laughter swelled.

After that Liza could do nothing but reach out, put her hand on the rusted door handle, and pull.

Chapter 18

Liza

THE CHOICE

The room was a bare, circular chamber, very brightly lit. For a minute Liza stood blinking, unused to such an unyielding brightness.

The first thing she noticed were the lightbulbs in the ceiling.

She wondered where the spindlers had gotten them, and where the wires for the electricity ran to, and pictured some poor family Above whose bills were always too high at the end of the month, and the father who would yell at the children about where all that power went—when really, of course, it was the spindlers that were the whole problem.

The second thing she noticed, after the lights, were the monsters.

And at that point, Liza stopped breathing.

On her left was some kind of a dog—except instead of having one head, it had three, and instead of having a normal tail, it had the tail of a scorpion.

On her right was a thing that Liza did not even have words for: like an octopus, except that it had hundreds of tentacles covered with glittering, razor-sharp spikes, and instead of a large, bulbous body it had a very small, narrow one, tapering to a pointed head and dominated by an overlarge single eye. The eye was turned to Liza and was staring at her.

Instinctively Liza drew back against the door. Except the door was not there anymore: Under her fingers she felt only rough stone. There was no longer any way out. She had no choice but to go forward.

The three-headed dog climbed to its feet and began to growl. Saliva dripped from its three sets of fangs and pattered onto the rock floor beneath its massive body.

The octopus-thing hefted a dozen of its tentacles into the air. Its spikes grated against the stone as it moved, leaving tiny, razor-thin indentations in their wake.

Liza's legs began to shake. She felt as though her whole body had turned into a wobble. But she forced herself to take a single step forward, and then another one. Perhaps, she reasoned, if she stayed in the very center of the room—perhaps she could somehow move very fast, and squeeze between them—perhaps they were less dangerous than they looked, and wouldn't attack. . . .

But no sooner had she taken her third step than suddenly the dog sprang and the octopus struck out with its spikes. Liza saw teeth and sharp, whipping legs cutting through the air toward her and fell backward, screaming.

Then, just as suddenly, the three-headed dog was jerked sharply backward and the octopus's tentacles carved a harmless arc in the air, just a few inches from Liza's skin.

Liza stood up cautiously, frowning. Now she saw something she hadn't noticed earlier. The three-headed dog had a collar around its neck, and the collar was attached to a thick iron chain that connected to a rusted stake driven into the ground. The octopus, too, was constrained: A metal ring was clamped tight around its narrow body, rooting it firmly in place.

That was why the dog had been jerked backward, and the octopus's tentacles had not reached her, and why the monsters did not merely rush at her as she stood by the place where the door had been.

They couldn't.

The three-headed dog continued to growl at her, and the octopus continued to wave its glittering, spike-covered tentacles threateningly, and Liza tried to think.

Thanks to the bright light in the chamber, she could make out the exact dimensions of the two monsters' restricted spaces. Over time, the octopus had been wearing away the rock, the way that a sculptor chisels into stone.

The dog's enclosure was slightly harder to see; but when Liza peered closely, she could make out another broad circle, absolutely clear of loose stones and bits of rock, gravel that had over time been kicked and swept away by the dog's endless pacing.

Two circles: and only three inches of space between them. It reminded Liza of the Venn diagrams she had had to study in art class, when she learned that by blending yellow and blue you could make green. Except that these circles were not quite touching.

Still, there was not enough space for a person to pass through. If she wished to avoid the octopus, she would have to step in reach of the three-headed dog. If she wished to avoid the three-headed dog, she would have to go within reach of the tentacles.

Of course, Liza thought. Despite her fear, she felt a rush of satisfaction. What had the queen said? *I, of course, have always liked tests, hurdles, riddles, puzzles, traps, and snares.* Of course it could not have been as simple as waltzing through three rooms. Of course there were bound to be tests and trials and tricks. There always were. Nothing was ever easy.

Perhaps, Liza thought, she could go *over* the two monsters . . . ? But she saw quickly that this was impossible. The walls were too slick for her to climb; there were no toe- or footholds to speak of.

But maybe the monsters were not as bad as they seemed. Maybe they only *looked* fearsome; maybe they were actually tame, like Mr. Peer's little mutt, who was always barking and growling at every passing car but was actually the gentlest dog you could imagine. You only had to hold out your hand and he would come and nuzzle you like a long-lost friend.

The idea filled Liza with renewed hope. Next to her was a pile of stones, roughly the size of softballs but much heavier; she hefted one up and, to test her theory, rolled it toward the three-headed dog.

"Come on, little puppy," she crooned, thinking that might help. "Play nice with the ball."

The three-headed dog sprang, snarling. As it leapt, its chain rattled terribly and the metal stake rooting the monster in place wobbled and shook, so that for one horrible second Liza thought it would be lifted clear out of the ground, and the three-headed dog would be free. It landed with its heavy paws around the stone, and the left-most head chomped right through the softball-size rock, sending gravel showering from its jaws, as though the stone was as thin as cardboard.

Liza swallowed. Tiny pebbles—now coated in the dog's greenish saliva—bounced back toward her feet.

"Now it's your turn, Mr. Octopus," she said. For some reason, speaking out loud made her feel better. It was like peering into a dark closet and announcing loudly to the monsters, *I know you're there, so don't even think about trying to jump out at me.* When you spoke to them directly, they never did. She released another stone in the octopus's direction, as though bowling.

Instantly the octopus shot out one of its tentacles, like a baseball player connecting hard with a fastball. The stone shattered on impact and went zinging into a thousand pieces all around the cavern. Liza ducked instinctively, covering her face, and felt a rush of air around her, like a dozen bullets had just zoomed past her.

There was a yelp and a roar; the rattle of a chain. Then a high, shrill scream. She looked up and saw that the three-headed dog was covered in welts where pieces of the shattered stone had hit it. Furious, the dog had gone for the octopus. It was baring all its enormous teeth, scorpion tail lashing, straining at the chain that kept it only an inch from the octopus's tentacles.

The octopus, in turn, was thrusting furiously with its tentacles, trying to strike out at the enraged animal, but it, too, could not reach, and it let out a howl of frustration every time one of its tentacles clanged harmlessly to the ground. Liza could see hatred burning in its single eye.

And it gave her an idea.

There were three heavy stones remaining. Liza picked up the first rock—the largest, heaviest one— in her right hand.

It is very, very difficult to step closer to an enraged dog; it is even harder to step closer to an enraged dog with three enraged heads; and it is almost impossible to step closer when you must also go closer to a many-tentacled monster that is shrieking and lashing with huge metal spikes. Liza forced her legs forward, feeling as though she was walking a tightrope and in danger of falling off.

As she neared the three-headed dog, its right head whipped in her direction and began snarling at her and baring its teeth, although thankfully its other heads remained fixed in the octopus's direction.

She stopped a few inches short of the faint line that marked the dog's circular enclosure. She was close enough that she could smell its foul breath. She could feel, too, the tentacles cutting the air behind her, whipping just a few short inches from her, and she could not help but imagine the solid rock, chomped or shattered into bits. It made her think of what the queen had done to the moribat.

"Focus," Liza said to herself. She lifted the stone like a bowler at the end of the alley, gripping it so tightly her knuckles turned white.

That was what Anna would tell her to do, what Anna had always told her to do when they played games of Pinecone Bowling. That was what she would do; she would pretend she was playing Pinecone Bowling at home, on the lawn, with Patrick and Anna.

Liza dropped quickly into a crouch and swung the rock forward forcefully, aiming for the metal stake in the ground just behind the dog's scorpion tail. The rock missed the stake by half an inch and bounced harmlessly, with a hollow thud, off the chamber's wall. The noise made yet another head swivel in her direction.

Liza felt her mouth go dry as dust.

That's okay, she imagined Anna saying. *You can try again.*

Liza lifted the second rock from its pile with a trembling hand. This one was slightly smaller than the last one.

Once again, she dropped into a kind of bowler's lunge, shooting the rock forward. It sped straight toward the metal stake and connected with a clang; Liza watched in both terror and exhilaration as the metal stake shuddered and tipped.

For a second the dog was given an extra inch of space on its chain, and it clawed forward, swiping at Liza and the octopus simultaneously, so Liza had to draw quickly back. Then the stake righted itself and the dog was jerked backward again, leaving claw marks etched in the dark rock and letting off a howl of frustration.

By this time all three heads were turned toward Liza, and the three-headed dog began to pace back and forth in its small circle, tail lashing furiously behind it. The octopus, too, had become increasingly agitated. All its hundreds of tentacles were raised now, metal spikes gleaming in the harsh light of the chamber. It reminded Liza of a stark black tree, covered all over with metal icicles.

Liza had only one rock remaining: the smallest and lightest rock, her very last chance.

She once again inched forward, to the very edge of the line that had been drawn faintly against the rock floor by the three-headed dog's endless pacing. She took a deep breath. She thought of Patrick.

She dropped into a crouch and released the rock with as much force as she could . . .

. . . and watched it skitter harmlessly past its mark, missing the metal stake by a good six inches.

The monster looked at her, and all three of its heads seemed to smile. Liza felt her stomach sink to her toes. She was out of chances—and out of ideas, too.

Then she remembered—Patrick's baseball! It was still nestled at the bottom of her pocket where she had placed it after retrieving it from Mirabella, along with Patrick's socks, her father's glasses, and a small collection of seeds of hope.

For the last time, Liza gripped the ball and shuffled

forward. *I can do this*, she told herself. *I will* do *it*.

The three-headed dog drew back all three of its mouths, showing tongues wet with saliva and fangs as sharp as knives.

Slowly it approached, snarling. She forced herself to stand still, even though every single muscle in her body was twitching and shaking and telling her to *run*. Closer, closer the monster came, taking its time now. For the moment, she was still standing just out of reach of its long, curved teeth and its powerful jaws; she was still safe.

But not for long.

And then, all at once, the monster pounced. At the same moment Liza dropped to her knees and rolled the baseball, hard, from her hands. The ball went straight and fast against its target.

For one second everything froze. The three-headed dog with its mouths open and roaring, ready to chomp her to bits, seemed to hover in midair almost directly above her.

Then the ancient stake, which had been keeping the monster rooted in place for longer than time has been an idea, popped out of the ground. And the three-headed dog, free of its leash, continued sailing, sailing, sailing—over Liza, who had flung herself onto her stomach and felt the heat from the dog's massive scorpion tail pass not an inch from her skin—and directly into the tangled mess of razor-sharp tentacles.

Everything exploded. The cavern was filled with horrible noise: barks and snarls and screams and clashing metal. Liza's head rang; her mouth was full of dust; her knees were cut and scraped from her hard fall to the ground. But she climbed to her feet and sprinted toward the door at the far side of the chamber, cutting through the three-headed dog's now-vacant circle.

She looked back only once, when she had reached the door and had already taken hold of the handle. She looked back toward the source of the terrible symphony of sound, which had swelled to a crescendo: the sound of thousands and thousands of years of pent-up anger and frustration, suddenly released.

For a moment she did not understand what she was seeing. There were heads and teeth and claws and thin, waving legs, but she could not tell where one monster began and the other ended. They were so locked in battle, biting and lashing and tearing at each other, that they seemed almost to have merged together.

They would destroy each other, Liza knew with

a sudden certainty. They would bite and tear and cut until there was nothing left of either of them; then the chamber would be empty, and it would be safe for her to return.

Liza had made it through the first room. She pushed open the door and stepped into the second.

Chapter 19

Patrick

THE HALL OF MIRRORS

As soon as the door swung closed behind her, the sounds of the monsters' battle were swallowed completely, and Liza was left in perfect silence. After the stark brightness of the first chamber, the second room seemed enormous, and full of shadows and strange reflections. For a moment she had an overwhelming feeling of vertigo and had to press up against the wall behind her for support. The door was once again gone. It had disappeared just as it had in the first room.

As her eyes adjusted to the dim blue light, she

realized why she felt so dizzy and disoriented.

The second room was full of mirrors.

The space was not as enormous as Liza had, at first, believed. Instead it was lined on either side with mirrored doors, all of them reflecting the shadows and the strange, flickering light, and then reflecting those reflections, and then reflecting the reflection of those reflections, on and on and on.

Unlike the first room, this one was old and damp. Stalactites dripped like candle wax from the uneven ceiling, and pools of moisture collected along the uneven ground. All this, too, was reflected.

Liza took a step forward and saw her own reflection appear in the first set of mirrors. She looked strange to herself: pale and much smaller than she looked in the mirrors at home. She wondered whether being underground had somehow shrunk her. How long had she been Below? It might have been days, or weeks. Liza could no longer tell.

"How strange," she said out loud, and of course, the two reflections spoke with her.

"But at least," she said to the two Lizas, "it's much better than the monsters." In fact, she did not see that this room was anything at all to be frightened of. One of these mirrored doors must, she reasoned, be the door that led to the third and final room; she would walk along the row and try them all.

She walked confidently toward the first door on her left. Then, from behind her, a voice spoke out.

"No, Liza!"

She spun around, her heart hammering. And there, standing in the third mirror on the right, was Patrick. He was shaking his head frantically and banging on the inside of the glass, as though he could force his way out of the mirror and into her side of the world.

Liza was so surprised she could hardly speak. "Is—is that really you?" she asked in a bare whisper. It didn't seem possible that after the long journey, and all the trials and troubles she had endured, she had finally found her brother.

Patrick nodded. For a moment Liza thought she saw a strange look pass across his face—a look of triumph—but then she was sure it was only a trick of the light.

"Yes, yes," he said eagerly. "It's really me. Come and open the door, so I can get out."

Liza started toward him.

"Don't listen to him! He's a liar!" a voice burst out behind her. She whirled around and saw a second Patrick, this one in the fourth mirror to the left. "I'm the real Patrick. Behind his door there is a snake the size of a train; he wants you to open up so you'll be eaten. It's one of the queen's tricks. Don't fall for it."

"You can't trust him," the first Patrick said, crossing his arms and jutting out his lower lip in a very Patrick way. "He's the one who's lying. Behind his door are a thousand hungry spindlers, waiting to devour you."

"They're both liars," came a third voice, and Liza, desperately confused, saw yet another Patrick step into yet another mirror. "I'm the real Patrick. Both of them work for the queen. If you open either of their doors, you'll be dead quicker than a fly in a toilet bowl."

"You're one to talk." A fourth Patrick appeared, snorting scornfully at the third Patrick. "You're hiding poisonous stingers behind your door. She'll be dead as a doornail before she's finished turning the handle. I'm the real Patrick, Liza."

"No, I am!" A fifth Patrick appeared.

"No, I am!" And a sixth.

More and more Patricks appeared in more and more mirrors—until the hall was full of them, and filled with the clamorous sounds of shouting as they hurled accusations at one another and begged Liza to open their door, the *real* door.

Liza's head was full of buzzing, and she was dizzier than ever. She walked back and forth between the rows of mirrors, panic welling inside her. She had no doubt that behind most of these doors some horrible evil was lying in wait. The queen of the spindlers would have made sure of that.

"Liza, over here!"

"Liza, over here!"

One of these doors *must* lead to the last room. But all the Patricks looked the same to her: They were dressed in the same ratty corduroys with the frayed cuffs, and the same faded BROOKLYN T-shirt, and the same red Chuck Taylors, just how the real Patrick would dress. And each of them pouted and shouted and snorted and stamped like the real Patrick did when he was throwing a tantrum.

"Don't listen to any of them, Liza! Open my door!"

"No! Open mine!"

"Stop it!" Liza gritted her teeth and clamped her hands over her ears. She couldn't think; the voices and the shouting were too loud. If they would only be quiet . . .

"There's a nest of hornets the size of softballs behind his door—"

"He's a liar, Liza! Come on! You can tell just by listening to him."

"Shut up!" Liza cried. "Shut up and let me think for a minute!"

But the Patricks did not shut up. If anything, their shouting grew louder, until the room echoed with voices and the stalactites trembled from the ceiling, and the water in the puddles was full of ripple and vibration. And it was just like the real Patrick not to listen, and do the exact reverse of what you wanted him to do.

"Liza!"

"Liza!"

"Liza!"

Liza's anger peaked, and she lashed out in frustration, driving her fist against the nearest mirror.

"I said shut up!" she cried; and felt a sharp ribbon of pain shoot from her hand all the way up her arm as she connected with the glass. A dark trickle of blood ran between her fingers, and she brought her hand quickly to her mouth. A web of fissures had appeared in the mirror, splintering Patrick's image into a hundred pieces. Still, he continued shouting at her, his mouth now a hundred mouths.

All the Patricks continued shouting at her.

All of them, that is, but one.

She had seen him out of the corner of her eye as her hand had cracked the glass. He had reached for her quickly, instinctively. And now he asked her, "Are you okay?"

Liza, no longer unsure, walked directly to the mirrored door in which the real Patrick was reflected, as all around her the clamor and shouting continued. Then she put both hands against the mirror and pushed; and she passed through, into the third and final room.

Chapter 20

Liza

THE FINAL TEST

O nce again Liza felt instantly disoriented; she appeared to have walked straight into a forest. The ground was carpeted in thick green moss, and large trees formed a vaulted ceiling over her head.

All around her were silver and gold flowers with blossoms the shape of tiny trumpets; the air smelled sweet and was full of birdsong. It was the most beautiful place Liza had ever seen. She heard laughter coming from somewhere beyond the trees; and she had just started to move toward the sound when a girl stepped out of the woods. As soon as she saw

Liza, her face lit up.

"Liza!" the girl said, and broke into a run. "I'm so glad you made it!" She seized both of Liza's hands in her own.

"I—I'm sorry," Liza said, feeling suddenly shy. "I don't think I know you."

The girl was the prettiest person Liza had ever seen, and seemed to match perfectly with the beauty of her surroundings. She was older—she must have been Anna's age, Liza thought, and in fact she kind of *looked* like Anna, except that instead of wearing jeans with dirty cuffs and an old band T-shirt as Anna usually did, this girl was wearing a dress that seemed to be made entirely of leaves and petals. But she had Anna's long blond hair and straight white teeth.

The main difference in their looks, Liza saw, was in the eyes: Anna had hazel eyes, while this girl's were the vivid green of the thick moss that grew beneath her bare feet.

The girl laughed. Her laughter reminded Liza of bells ringing on a clear day. "Don't be silly," she said. "Don't tell me you don't know your own sister."

"Sister?" Liza croaked out.

"*Forever* sister," the girl said happily, as she began tugging Liza forward into the trees. "The others didn't think you would make it. Of course, I knew you would.

I hoped you would, at least. And you did! We'll have a party; we'll get cupcakes. Do you like cupcakes? Of course you do. . . ."

"Wait," Liza said. "You don't understand. I don't have very much time—"

The girl cut her off with another tinkling laugh. "Time is all we have!" she said. "There's loads and loads of it here."

They emerged into a clearing. A large table was set up underneath a white silken canopy, which was hung all over with twinkling lights. The clearing was carpeted with tiny flowers of all different colors, and Liza's bare feet sank into the soft petals as she walked.

There was something familiar about the table in the clearing, although it took Liza a moment to realize what it was. Then she got it: The table looked very much like the kitchen table at home, and had four chairs just as her table did, although everything here was larger and grander. There was, for example, no stack of coasters wedged under the second table leg, to keep it from wobbling; and none of the plates were webbed with cracks, as they were at home.

There were three people sitting at the table, feasting on food served from enormous platters: a man, with gray hair and kind-looking eyes; across from him, laughing, a woman, with the older girl's long blond hair and a cape of flowers draped over her shoulders; a boy, probably Patrick's age, with red cheeks, a crown of golden curls, and wide, smiling eyes.

All three of them turned as Liza entered the clearing, and even though they nodded and smiled welcomingly, Liza hung back, feeling shy again.

"She's here!" the-girl-who-looked-like-Anna said triumphantly. "Didn't I say she would come?"

"Welcome home, Liza," the woman said. She was as beautiful as her daughter: Warmth seemed to emanate from her eyes, filling Liza with a bubbly happiness from her toes to her head.

"This—this isn't home," Liza stuttered.

"Of course it is," the older woman said, laughing. "It's your new home. We've been waiting for you! And now everything is just as it should be at last."

"Exactly so," said the gray-haired man heartily. "From now on there will be nothing but happiness!"

"And games," the little boy with the smiling eyes put in.

"And parties," the-girl-who-looked-like-Anna said, squeezing Liza's hand excitedly. "And laughter all the time!"

"And love, of course," added the older woman

gently. "We will always love one another."

"Let's toast!" said the man. He lifted his glass.

"Come on, Liza," said the-girl-who-looked-like-Anna. "Sit and toast with us."

The bubbly feeling had made all the pain and fear of Liza's journey underground begin to unloosen, and she was desperately tempted to sit down. But she could not forget about Patrick—not when she had come this far.

She said, with some regret in her voice, "I can't. I must find Patrick. I must rescue my brother." Seeing the gray-haired man frown, she quickly added, "But maybe on the way back? Patrick would like it here too. He loves games."

"That won't do," said the gray-haired man, with a shake of his head.

"Not at all," his wife trilled.

The-girl-who-looked-like-Anna slipped an arm around Liza's shoulders. Her skin smelled sweet, like honeysuckle and raspberry.

"I don't understand," she said, in her sweetest voice. "Don't you want to stay here and be sisters?"

"Yes," Liza answered truthfully.

"And don't you want to be happy forever?" the-girl-who-looked-like-Anna asked.

"Yes," Liza said. "Of course."

"Then you must forget about Patrick," the girl crooned, and she once again drew Liza to the table. "You must forget about everything that came before, and sit and eat with us; and then you will have everything you've ever wanted, and you and I will spend all of forever never growing up, and being beautiful and young and loved and happy."

Liza looked at the four smiling faces at the table, perfectly happy, perfectly harmonious, like four well-sounded notes on a piano. She swallowed hard.

"But—" she said. "But I can't stay here forever. I have to return Above."

"Above!" the-girl-who-looked-like-Anna scoffed, and even the way she pronounced the word made it sound small and dirty and unappealing, like a tiny room with no windows. "What could you possibly want from Above?"

Suddenly Liza had a hard time remembering. She thought of her own kitchen table; she thought of her father's distracted mutterings and the sound of her mother pacing, pacing back and forth. She stammered out, "My mom and dad are Above. If I stay here, they'll worry about me."

"Will they?" the older woman asked, arching an eyebrow.

"Are you sure about that?" The gray-haired man smiled widely.

"And are they always happy?" the-girl-who-looked-like-Anna said. "And do they always love you?"

Liza thought of the exclamation point between her mother's eyebrows, and her mother telling her to *be a good girl and act your age*, and *stay quiet so Mommy can think*; and her father, who worked all the time and then came home too tired to talk or play. She drew the chair out a little farther from the table so that she could sit down.

"She sits!" cried the gray-haired man.

"Hooray for Liza!" the boy said, bouncing in his seat.

"My lovely girl!" said the older woman.

"My forever sister!" the-girl-who-was-even-prettier-than-Anna said, her eyes flashing an almost electric green.

Liza froze just as she was about to lower herself into the chair. Just that—that momentary flash of green in the girl's eyes—had reminded her of the spindlers' eyes watching her from the dark. She thought, too, of the scawgs; they also had laid a feast for her. With a tremendous effort, she wrenched her hand from the chair and took one step away from the table.

"You are not real," she said, and the words, too, took a great effort.

The gray-haired man laughed, but to Liza's ears, his laughter sounded forced. "What do you mean?"

"The table, the birds, the forest—" Liza pointed to each thing in turn. "None of it is real."

"Liza." The-girl-who-looked-like-Anna came and gripped Liza tightly by the shoulders. "Liza, listen to me. I will be your bravest, brightest, most lovingest sister. Don't you want to stay with me?"

Her words tugged at Liza's soul, drawing her back to the table. It took all her strength to resist. "I can't," she said.

The girl released Liza's shoulders abruptly. "There is nothing for you Above," she said angrily. "Nothing but dullness and drudgery, and homework and fighting, and mashed peas and people who won't give you what you want. Here everything is perfect, and you will always have everything exactly to your liking, and you will always be happy."

Her voice was a thick syrup in Liza's brain. It was so hard to think. But she fought her way through it. "It's no big trick to be happy when everything is perfect," she said slowly. "And it isn't brave, either. Anyone can do that."

"And what does it matter what is real and what

isn't?" the-girl-who-looked-like-Anna said, her voice rising hysterically. "You believe in us, and that is real enough."

But it was too late. Liza had taken another step away from the table, and another. And as she did the gray-haired man, the beautiful older woman, the boy, and the Anna-who-was-not-really-Anna—all of them seemed to grow fuzzier, blurrier, like a TV image fading away into static.

"Yes, but Patrick believes in *me*," she said. "And that is *very* real."

The almost-Anna let out a mangled cry and ran at Liza, arms outstretched, her eyes growing to huge half crescents: spindler eyes. Liza felt a tremendous rush of air, a current blowing all around her, and suddenly the woods were full of shrieking, and all the birds took off into the sky at once, a swollen black cloud, and Liza felt as though she would be sucked up into the hurricane of noise and tearing. She was terrified, and so she closed her eyes and listed all the things she knew to be real and true, loudly, over the wind and the roaring:

"Mom likes rye toast in the morning. Dad takes his coffee without milk. Patrick does not like the feeling of wet feet on the grass and must have his sandals lined up next to the pool. My favorite color is red. On the bedside table are three purple hair clips, given to me by Aunt Elizabeth."

The roaring noise around her reached a crescendo, and Liza felt icy hands gripping her wrists, nearly pulling her off her feet.

She yelled out, "Summer comes after spring, and autumn comes after summer, and after winter, spring will come again."

Suddenly the noise fell away completely. Liza cracked one eye open, and then the other.

She was standing in a perfectly plain white room, completely silent, completely bare. The forest, the trees, the table—all of it was gone. There was a plain wooden door set in one wall.

Liza walked across the room and opened it, and so she left the third and final room, and at last she reached her brother in the Web of Souls.

Chapter 21

THE WEB

Liza stood in a vast, dark space in front of a web the size of a towering building; it stretched up and up and up into the mist and the gloom, trembling slightly in the cool, dank currents of air that swirled through the cavern.

The web was spun with silver thread that glinted and glittered and seemed to give off its own, cold light.

Up and up and up: loops and curlicues, spun silken strands.

She took one step toward the web, and then

another. It reminded her of being very small and going with her parents to New York City: the terrible towers of metal and glass! The rivers and waterfalls of concrete! The enormous tongues of stone and brick, wagging from the sky, as though ready to swallow you.

The Web of Souls was like that, but bigger and more terrible.

And what made it most terrible—beautiful and frightening all at once—were the souls, the hundreds and hundreds of souls, glowing and pulsing among its sticky strands. She *knew* that was what they were, immediately and without question, although the souls did not look exactly as she had imagined they would.

They were colored, first of all. Each soul was wrapped in a cocoon of silver thread, which bound it tightly to the web: But even so, the colors showed through, faintly, a haze of different hues. Some souls glowed bright orange, others were the shade of dusky twilight, others were a pure blue, others shone in colors Liza did not have a name for, so the whole effect of standing before the Web of Souls was like staring up at the world's largest Christmas tree.

The second surprising thing was their size. They were small. Even the largest was no bigger than a softball, and some were closer to the size of a Ping-Pong ball or smaller.

And yet, out of all the hundreds of souls that Liza could see—so many, Liza did not see how she could possibly carry all of them Above—she recognized Patrick's soul right away. She did not even have to think about it. She just knew.

(How do you explain this? It is a great mystery, and one that the lumer-lumpen might perhaps know how to answer. But the lumpen are not speaking, so a mystery it will no doubt remain.)

Patrick's soul was about the size of a lumpy softball, and it was for the most part a comforting maroon color, like the color of the well-worn fleece blanket at the foot of Liza's bed, although in tiny places it appeared much closer to a fire-engine red, and in others a deep ink-purple. It was hanging just off to Liza's left, a little bit higher than eye level, and as she approached it a great feeling of relief and joy swept through her. For the first time since coming Below, she let a single tear fall to the ground.

"Hi, Patrick," she whispered, and it seemed to her that just for a moment the soul flared slightly brighter. "I'm here to take you home."

That was when the ground underneath her gave a gigantic heave.

Liza stumbled, cried out, and unconsciously grabbed the web to steady herself. Pain ripped through her palm, and she withdrew her hand quickly. The strands of the web were hard, and hot, and very sharp, like razor wire. There was now a long, thin cut across Liza's palm, dotted with bright red beads of blood.

Fear yawned open inside her as the ground continued to buckle and roll, as though the whole underworld was a wet dog trying to shake itself dry. Across the cavern, an enormous stone came crashing down from the ceiling, splintering to pieces and sending another shudder through the ground. It made Liza's teeth rattle in her head. Her heart was a constant hum, a tremor. . . .

And then she felt it, beating there under her heart: the black brush-tip of wings.

Hello, said her nocturna, quite calmly, and for a moment she saw its wise black eyes hovering in front of her face.

"You found me!" Liza was so relieved, she nearly let another tear fall.

Of course I found you. I told you I would be watching.

But how?

I am always with you, Liza.

The ground heaved enormously, sending Liza

tumbling, hard, onto her backside. "What's happening?" she cried out.

Listen to me, Liza. There isn't much time.

Another rock, the size of a boulder, came hurtling down from above; Liza watched in horror as it took out a whole portion of the web, burying a dozen souls in rubble and debris. More rocks came raining down; the cavern was filling with a gray, choking dust.

I don't understand. Is this an earthquake?

It's the queen. Her nocturna's voice was grim. *She is furious that you made it past her traps. She is tearing down the nests.*

For a moment Liza's heart stopped beating entirely, and in that moment she could feel the nocturna's vibrations, which were nestled like a shadow on the other side of her heart.

What do you mean?

I mean she is planning to bury you here, at the Web of Souls.

Crash! Another boulder landed not four feet away from Liza. Panic rose inside her and she scrambled to her feet, tipping and dipping as the floor continued to sway.

Quick, Liza! You must work quickly.

Liza sprang forward and reached for Patrick's soul. Her hands were shaking as she tried to detach

219

the tiny glowing shape from the threads encasing it.

But it was like trying to pull an egg through the narrow bars of an iron cage without breaking it; the spindler web bit painfully into her fingers and hands and would not allow her to wrestle Patrick's soul free. Rocks continued to crash down all around her, tearing holes in the web, crushing souls beneath their weight.

Hurry, Liza!

"I can't!" Panic and terror made Liza shout out loud, and turned her clumsy. The next buckle of the ground sent her tumbling away from the web. She landed on her right wrist and felt it twist painfully underneath her. "His soul is stuck! They're all stuck!"

We have to go! More rocks; more red dust. *You'll have to leave him!*

"I can't leave him!" Liza was screaming now, over the echoing and the crashing and the sounds of splintering rock. She crawled back toward the web. The ground was a bull trying to buck her off its back, and she could barely climb to her feet. She tore at the web, trying to break apart the strands, mindless of the terrible pain in her hands, but it was like trying to rip apart pieces of metal. She could not hope to break through it.

And then there was another rumbling: a tumbling, swelling sound, as of distant thunder, terrifying, growing louder.

Liza! We have to go now!

I. Won't. Leave. Him! She continued to work fumblingly to tear Patrick's soul from the web, knowing it was hopeless.

Liza . . . the nocturna's voice sounded warningly, as the thunder grew louder.

No—not thunder. Feet. Something—many somethings—were coming toward her, and Liza allowed herself one fearful look over her shoulder.

And then, suddenly, the rats came swarming out of the darkness. Thousands and thousands of them, a roiling, mobile mass of black: and at the front of the herd, wearing not a single stitch of clothing, or a single spot of makeup, was Mirabella.

"Mirabella!" Liza, amazed, stepped back from the web. The rats rushed past her. They sprang onto the web; they swarmed it, they leapt and climbed and swung up its steep architecture. They nibbled and tore at its strands with their sharp teeth and their claws, and the cavern was filled with snapping and cracking, as the web began to come apart, and the souls began to loosen from their cocoons.

Mirabella paused briefly in front of Liza. Her

eyes were full of regret.

"I was a terrible friend," Mirabella whispered. But now that she was without the odd clothing and the face powder, the strangeness of her voice did not seem so strange; she sounded just the way a rat should. "I am sorry, Miss Liza. Will you forgive me?"

She did not wait for Liza to answer. She sprang for the web, heading straight for Patrick's soul. And she set to work chewing and nibbling her way around it, so that the strands encasing it, keeping it locked into the web, began to break away.

Crash! Crash! Liza ducked as more stones came raining furiously from above. A rock the size of a grapefruit hit her on the elbow, and she felt the impact through every nerve in her body. The nocturna's whirling had become so fast, and the pounding of Liza's heart such a furious echo of it, she was sure she would have a heart attack and die right there.

"Call up the nocturni!" Mirabella yelled. "The souls are coming loose!"

They're coming, Liza's nocturna said. *They don't need to be called.*

As the enormous, vaulted cavern fell to pieces around them, and the rats worked to free the souls in the web, and Liza stood amazed and terrified, and the ground continued to heave and roll as though the stone had been turned to frenzied ocean, from all over the dark corners of Below, the nocturni heard the sounds of souls released from their webbed cages, and they came.

They came out of the mist and the shadow—they *were* shadow—and in the middle of all the chaos and destruction even the rats stopped to watch. The nocturni floated and glided and seemed to materialize out of nothing; and as the souls began to drop from the web, like apples shaken from a tree, they were quickly taken up by their nocturni: eternal pairs, bonds that would never be broken.

Nocturni swooped through the air, carrying souls of different sizes and colors on their backs, between their wings. They disappeared into the mist again, so the air pulsed with the twinkling colored lights of souls receding into the distance. The nocturni would bring them home, Above, where they belonged.

Snap! Mirabella tore through the last threads keeping Patrick's soul pinioned to the spindlers' massive web, and his soul was released. Liza stretched out her arms to catch it as it floated—surprisingly gently, as though it weighed no more than a feather—toward the ground. Before she could grab it, however, a nocturna materialized out of the air and swept Patrick's soul neatly onto its back. Patrick's nocturna was slightly smaller than Liza's, although its wings were larger, and shaped almost like palm fronds.

Patrick's nocturna turned a circle around Liza. She could hear its voice beating to her through the air, but only faintly.

I'm sorry, Liza, Patrick's nocturna whispered. *I should have been keeping watch. It will never happen again.*

"That's all—," Liza started to say, but broke off as another rock came hurtling toward her from above. She fell to one side, rolling to safety, coughing up dust.

Let's go! Liza's nocturna screamed, as from above the remains of the web began to teeter, and groan, and tip, like a great metal tree about to be felled. Boulders continued to crash on all sides of them. Liza scrambled to her feet. *The web is falling! The nests are caving in!*

Liza could no longer see the way out. The rocks had made everything unfamiliar, and she could not remember which way she had come, or see any kind of door. She ran blindly, panicked, as black shapes swooped around her head and bits of the web—sharp and thin as needles—began to splinter off and crash all around her, a terrible, piercing rain. She went tumbling to her knees again as the ground gave another tremendous buckle.

"Here, Miss Liza." Mirabella was next to her then, and holding out a paw. "Get on my back. We'll move faster that way."

Liza took her paw gratefully and slid onto Mirabella's furry back, keeping her arms and legs locked tightly around the rat's body so she would not fall off. The other rats were a moving, pumping blur of bodies around them; and above them, the dark cloud of nocturni swept through the air.

Hurry! Hurry! She's coming down!

With a thunderous noise, the remains of the web came crashing to the ground, sending daggers of hard thread spinning in every direction. Liza felt them whizzing through the air like arrows. An enormous rock was blocking their way. They would never make it; they would be pierced to death by sharp metal points.

"Hold on!" Mirabella cried.

At the last second the rat leapt. Liza grabbed her fur tightly, and then they were soaring, skimming over the rock, and slamming down on the other side, sliding into a dark, narrow tunnel. The cavern receded behind them as the last bit of the Web of Souls came crashing to the earth.

Liza looked to her left; Patrick's nocturna was flying next to her, with Patrick's soul nestled safely between its wings; and she could feel her own nocturna flying close to her right shoulder, its wings just brushing her skin. They were surrounded by black everywhere: rats, nocturni, all in a panic, drumming through the tunnel. This, too, was shaking and trembling and coming down around them; Liza knew the queen did not intend to let her leave the nests alive.

"Light!" roared Mirabella. And then, "For lumpen's sake, this is no time for formality! Illuminate! Illuminate!"

Greenish light filled the twisting tunnel, as the lumer-lumpen began to emit their pulsing radiance. In the light, the black backs of the rats looked like a tumbling river of oil.

That was when the moribats came.

They came screeching, filling the tunnel with their terrible noise, talons extended, eyes bloodshot and glowing red against the pallor of their featherless, beaked faces. Liza saw that they were diving for the souls; they clutched at the glowing, colored

226

shapes, swatting at the nocturni with their enormous wingtips. Liza watched, horrified, as one nocturna was sent, skittering, against the cavern wall; the soul it was carrying fell and cracked on the ground like an overripe fruit, revealing a glittering purple interior. Then it was stomped to pieces as the rats swarmed over it.

As the moribats came flapping through the tumbling-down tunnel, dodging old stones and stalactites shaken loose by the rolling, buckling ground, more nocturni rose up to meet them. They formed protective clouds around the soul-carriers and helped to beat the moribats away, so the air was filled with twisting black and white shapes, blurring together. Liza watched as a spinning cloud of black enveloped an attacking moribat; then the moribat was falling, lifeless, with a *thump*, and they were running past it.

Thump! Thump! Thump! Nocturni, working together, began to take down the moribats one by one.

The tunnel widened, and opened into the cavernous room where Liza had met with the queen. This, too, had begun to collapse, and was filled with crumbling mounds of rock, enormous hills of shale and glittering quartz, and mist. There was no sign of the spindlers. They were gone.

The screams of the moribats, and the thumping of the dead, receded behind them—and still Liza saw colored shapes bobbing up and away, as the soul-bearing nocturni flew up into the swirling mist and darkness. She hoped they would make it safely Above.

A narrow tunnel was lit up with a greenish glow on Mirabella's right.

"Hang on!" the rat screamed, and veered sharply toward it at the last second, nearly sending Liza flying. Mirabella's claws screeched against the stone as they slipped and slid into the narrow space.

Is the rat sure about this? Liza's nocturna panted out, and Liza could hear that it was tiring.

Liza folded Mirabella's large ear back toward her and spoke into it as though into a megaphone. "Are you sure this is the right way?" This tunnel was so narrow, Liza had to press herself nearly flat and keep her head ducked low to keep from bumping against the globe-encased lumpen suspended from the ceiling above her. Her nostrils were full of the musky smell of Mirabella's fur.

"The lumpen always show the correct path," Mirabella panted back. Liza could feel the rat's muscles straining underneath her.

For a brief second, Liza allowed herself to wonder whether she ought to be trusting Mirabella. She thought of what the queen had said, that a rat is a rat, and nothing more, and nothing ever changed.

But no. Something *had* changed. Mirabella had come back for her; Mirabella had freed Patrick's soul.

And, in fact, the narrow tunnel appeared to be sloping gently upward, and from ahead came the unmistakable singsong voices of the River of Knowledge. And as the tunnel around them gave a terrible shudder, and large cracks began to form, weblike, along its sides and ceiling, Mirabella, Liza, and the two nocturni burst out onto the muddy banks of the river.

Liza slid off Mirabella's back as the rat collapsed, exhausted, onto its haunches.

"You did it!" she said, and once again wrapped Mirabella in a tight hug. The rat's whiskers tickled her neck. "You saved us!"

"Not so fast," rasped a voice behind them.

Liza whirled around. The queen of the spindlers dropped clumsily to the ground from above the mouth of the tunnel, where she must have been waiting for them to emerge.

Two of her legs appeared to be broken, and she was coated with a thick black substance that looked like blood. She had not escaped the falling shards of rock unharmed. Still, she swelled herself to an enormous size, towering above Liza, Mirabella, and the two fluttering nocturni, casting them all in dark shadow.

"That soul belongs to me," she gasped out, raising a trembling finger. "You will not take it from here. You will not escape; your soul, and his, will be my feed."

The queen swayed, shut her crescent eyes, and then regained control. When she opened her eyes again, they were full of a black, burning hatred, and Liza was so scared she couldn't move, or breathe.

"Stay away from Miss Liza," Mirabella said gallantly, puffing out her chest, although her voice cracked and squeaked with terror.

"Shut up, you useless creature." The queen swatted at Mirabella almost absentmindedly with one of her enormous arms and sent the rat flying. Mirabella thumped to the ground with a groan and a whimper, twenty feet away. She tried to stand, then collapsed into the dirt again.

"You must let us go!" Liza cried, stuttering a little. "I passed through the rooms. I beat all your stupid tests. I won Patrick's soul back, fair and square."

"Fair?" the queen parroted shrilly. Black venom

dripped from her fangs. "Fair? You sniveling little idiot—nothing in the whole universe, either Above or Below, is ever fair."

"But you said—," Liza began. She was cut off by the queen's raucous, hoarse laughter.

"I know what I said." The queen sneered at her.

"You lied to me." Liza balled her fists. She could feel Patrick's nocturna hovering behind her, and Patrick's soul emitting a faint heat, and it made her feel brave.

"Are you so eager for the truth, then?" The queen swelled and swelled, towering, looming. "All right then, dearie. Here is the truth: Your souls belong to me, now and forever."

At that moment, the queen sprang. At the same time there was a tremendous cracking—like a thousand thunderbolts sounding at once—and Liza closed her eyes and prepared to die. Strangely, in that moment, she was not even afraid. She heard a scream and a cascade of tumbling stone; she wondered for a confused second whether it was she who was screaming.

Perhaps I am already dead, she thought.

Don't be ridiculous, her nocturna spoke. *Of course you're not dead.*

Liza, surprised, opened her eyes. Where there had once been a tunnel opening there was now an enormous pile of stone and rubble, and the only sign of the queen was a single, twitching hand, which protruded from underneath the rock.

The tunnel had collapsed, burying the queen of the spindlers underneath it.

That was close, Liza's nocturna said.

"I think," Liza said, tearing her eyes from the sight of the fluttering fingers and the sharp nails, "I very much think it is time to go home now."

From farther down the embankment, she heard a moan.

"Mirabella!" Liza cried. Mirabella was sitting up, rubbing her head. Liza ran to her, dropping to her knees in the black sand and gripping the rat tightly by the shoulders. "Are you all right?"

"No need to shout," Mirabella groaned, although Liza was speaking at a perfectly normal volume. There was a large, circular bump forming just between her ears.

"Come on," Liza said. "Let me help you up." She stood and offered her hand to Mirabella: Palm to paw, she got her friend to her feet.

"Can you walk?" Liza asked. "Have you broken anything?"

Mirabella felt her ribs gingerly, then examined the length of her tail. She shook her head.

"You'd better lean on me, just in case," Liza said.

So Mirabella slung one arm over Liza's shoulder, and Liza helped support her as they made their way slowly, painstakingly, out of the underworld: the rat, the girl, the two dark shapes of the nocturni, and a small soul glowing among them, giving them light.

Chapter 22

Liza

THE RETURN

Liza woke to the sound of voices downstairs. She was in her own bed. Sunlight was streaming through the thin paper blinds that covered her windows. It was another beautiful spring day.

"Are you *sure* you couldn't have left them at work?" she heard her mother say, and she knew her father still had not found his glasses.

His glasses! Suddenly it all came flooding back: the spindlers, the journey to the underworld, the long and winding way back. . . .

She sat up, and the room seemed to seesaw. There

was the taste of sand in the back of her throat; she must have swallowed a half gallon of water when she had almost drowned in the River of Knowledge.

She stood up, testing herself on her feet. She examined herself for bruises. But no—everything looked fine. Even her clothes appeared undamaged, and very clean. She patted her pockets and felt her heart sink. Her father's glasses were gone. For a second she was horribly and bitterly disappointed, thinking that the whole thing—all of Below—had been a dream.

But no. It must be real. She remembered the end of the journey in bits and pieces—she remembered supporting Mirabella and then, at a certain point, growing tired herself. She remembered a large barge hung with lights, and her nocturna's voice saying, *It's okay, Liza. Go ahead and sleep. We'll take you up the river.*

She did not remember coming up from the basement. She did not know how long she had been away. And she did not know what had happened to Patrick's soul.

Quickly Liza went to the door and stepped out into the hallway. She could hear a clock ticking. She could hear no sounds of sobbing, no indication that her parents had spent sleepless nights waiting for her to return. Was it possible—was it remotely possible—that she had gone Below, and returned, in only a single night?

She crossed to Patrick's room and cracked open the door. He was sleeping on his side, in a tangle of sheets, snoring a little bit. A small puddle of drool had formed on his pillow, and Liza felt her heart soar.

She crept close to the bed, leaning over him. Yes. She was almost positive that he was back.

"Patrick," she whispered, to be sure, and then said a little louder, shaking his shoulder, "Patrick."

Patrick's eyes opened. He yawned widely and pawed his eyes with two balled-up fists.

"I'm hungry," he said, and Liza felt a wave of joy break over her.

"We can have pancakes today. I'll make them," Liza said.

He made a face. "Ew," he said. "Your breath stinks."

He was back. So it had not been a dream. It was real—every last bit of it.

"Get dressed," Liza said, stepping away from the bed. "Today will be full of adventure."

"Can we have pancakes first?"

"If you brush your hair," Liza said, and Patrick grumbled a yes and slid out of bed.

Liza returned to her room, happier than she could

ever remember being. She took out her jean shorts and a favorite T-shirt, then thought better of it and removed a yellow sundress from her closet. Today was a special day.

As she was stepping out of her pajama bottoms, she heard a quiet pinging sound, like sand running through an hourglass. A small pile of seeds of hope had been shaken out of her pocket and lay scattered across the floorboards. Once again, she was filled with a sense of joy.

Mirabella was real. The lumpen were real. The nocturni and the nids and the mole conductor were real, and so were the terrible things too—the Court of Stones and the spindlers and morihats and the live forest, and the River of Knowledge, both gorgeous and deadly.

Liza stooped down to collect the seeds of hope carefully. As she did, she caught a glimpse of something on her nightstand, half-hidden under the balled-up sock she had retrieved from Mirabella: her father's glasses! She must have removed them from her pocket before she crawled into bed. Her heart seemed to triple in size. She put the seeds of hope in the pocket of her sundress and took up her father's glasses.

Downstairs, her mother was sitting in the kitchen, staring off into space, with a pile of bills heaped in front of her. She sat with her hands folded in her lap, and the small exclamation point was already there between her eyebrows. Her toast was untouched, and she was very pale.

"Patrick wants pancakes," Liza said, coming into the kitchen.

Her mother started, as though waking up from a dream.

"Not today, Liza," she said, and she sounded tired. "I've just run the dishwasher."

"But it's a special day," Liza insisted. "Patrick's soul has come back from the underworld. His nocturna carried it up."

"His what?"

"Nocturna. They're like little butterflies, and they bring dreams. They bring seeds of hope to the surface, too. And they're eternal. And there's one for every person in the whole world. Can you believe it?" Liza was filled with such a bubbly happiness, she did not notice her mother's face drooping and drooping, like rain melting down a windowpane.

"Oh, Liza!" Mrs. Elston suddenly cried. "What will I do with you!" And suddenly, to Liza's horror, her mother leaned her elbows on the table, put her face in her hands, and began to cry.

For a moment Liza stood paralyzed; she had never

seen her mother cry before, and the experience made something open inside her, something that made her feel very old. It was like seeing the River of Knowledge for the first time; she was filled with sadness and wonder both.

Liza approached the kitchen table. She reached into her pocket and selected two seeds of hope. She held them out to her mother.

"Do you know what these are?" she said gently, as though she was speaking to Patrick after one of his nightmares. "These are seeds of hope. They may not look like much, but they grow everywhere, in even the hardest places, where nothing else grows."

Mrs. Elston, sniffling, lifted her head from her hands and looked at her daughter. "Liza," she said.

"It's not a story, Mom. It's true. Go on." Liza offered up the seeds. "Take them. They're for you."

Mrs. Elston looked at the small dark seeds glinting in Liza's palm. She looked up at her daughter. She opened her mouth and closed it. Then she looked back at the seeds. And perhaps she saw the way that they flashed, momentarily brilliant; or perhaps she saw something else. In any case, she reached out and took the seeds in her own hand, and closed her fist tightly.

"Thank you," she said. Leaning forward suddenly,

she wrapped Liza in a fierce hug. "You know I love you, right? I love you and Patrick very much."

"You're squishing me," Liza said into her mother's shoulder. Mrs. Elston laughed and released her.

"And look," Liza said, placing her father's glasses on the table.

Mrs. Elston let out a cry of surprise. "Where did you *find* these?" she said. "Your father has been looking everywhere for them."

Liza thought about telling her mom about the troglod market, but at the last minute decided that she would let the troglods, and the nids, and Mirabella, be her secret—her secret and Patrick's, of course, since she could hardly *wait* to tell him. So she just said, "They were on my nightstand."

"You're a miracle, Liza," Mrs. Elston said, and leaned forward and kissed Liza on the middle of her forehead. "Your father went to look for them at the office. He'll be so relieved. I'll call him to tell him he can turn around and come home."

Bump, bump, bump. The real Patrick came down the stairs, sliding on his rump, with his hair squished flat against his forehead. "I'm ready," he said. "Where are the pancakes?"

"Mom said—," Liza began, but Mrs. Elston cut her off.

"I'll make the pancakes," she said, standing. "I think we even have a few chocolate chips left over. How does that sound? You go outside and play. I'll call you when they're ready."

"Pancakes! Pancakes! Pancakes!" Patrick shouted, as he ran for the door.

"Go on," Mrs. Elston said to Liza, smiling. The exclamation point hadn't totally disappeared, but it was much fainter now. "It'll be fifteen minutes at least."

When Liza was almost at the front door, Mrs. Elston called her back.

"I almost forgot," she said, shuffling through the pile of letters and half-crumpled envelopes on the kitchen table. "This came for you yesterday."

It was a postcard that showed an enormous red-brick building, half-covered in a thick green shag of ivy, like a vertical carpet. Liza's heart gave a flip, as though her nocturna had just brushed it with its wingtips.

On the back of the postcard was a note written in neat purple pen. It said:

Hey, Lizard—
How are you? College is awesome, but I miss you like crazy, of course. Can't wait to see you

when I'm home this summer. Have you seen On the Floor *yet? I'm totally going to take you. (Remember that time Patrick stuck all that popcorn in his nose?) Hope you've been working on your Pinecone Bowling skills, because otherwise,* PREPARE TO GET CREAMED.

xoxo

Anna

P.S. Tell Peapod I send him love and a hug.

Liza looked up at her mother. "Anna's coming home!" she burst out. She felt like she was rising and rising on a tide of joy. She had known it would be a special day today. She had felt it.

"Of course she is, sweet pea." Mrs. Elston smiled at her daughter. "How could she ever stay away from you?"

"Liza!" Patrick called to her from outside. He pressed his nose and hands against the screen door, and for a moment, when he withdrew, a brief impression of his image remained.

"Coming," she said. She tucked the postcard into her sundress pocket, so that it was nestled next to the seeds of hope, and followed Patrick outside.

Chapter 23

Patrick

A BIT OF MAGIC

Patrick was standing in the yard, trying to peer through the evergreen tree.

"See anything good?" Liza asked, coming toward him.

He turned to her and made a face. "Just a garden gnome," he said. "Nothing special."

"It was probably a troglod," Liza said. She came down the porch steps.

"A troglod?" Patrick raised his eyebrows.

"Uh-huh. Gnomes like cold temperatures, just like Anna said. It's mostly troglods that live around here. We'll have to remember to tell Anna when she comes home. She *is* coming home soon, did you know that?"

Patrick made a whooping sound and did his version of a victory dance, which involved clenching his fists and trying to shake the rest of his body into motion, and made him look a little like a cross between a jackhammer and a jellyfish.

"Troglods are crazy for pinks, of course," Liza said. "Maybe I'll get some for Mirabella—that's a rat I met, you know, when I was Below. I'm thinking I'll get her a real hat, too, and a new purse, since she lost hers in the Live Forest."

"She can have my Rangers hat," Patrick volunteered. Liza felt a rush of feeling for him that was as deep and layered and swirly as the River of Knowledge. Patrick always understood.

"That would be perfect," Liza said. "And you can help me cut up the pinks today, but only if you agree to be careful with the scissors."

Patrick made a farting noise by blowing air out of his cheeks, and Liza knew that this was his way of agreeing.

"And look what else," she said, and showed him the seeds of hope she had in her pocket. She did not, however, tell him that she had rescued his soul from the spindlers; not yet. That would come. "They're magic."

"They don't *look* it," Patrick said doubtfully.

"Oh, but they are," Liza said. "Very magic. There's lots of magic everywhere, you know."

And it was true: There was. From farther down the street, a lawn mower kicked into gear. The air was full of the smells of grass shavings and flowers, raindrops and damp towels, pancakes and rubber tires. Across the street, in Mr. and Mrs. Richardson's yard, several daffodils nodded in the breeze. Liza thought of the nids and wondered whether they would allow the rats and the troglods back into their balls, now that the spindlers were gone. She hoped so.

"Let's go give a seed to Mrs. Costenblatt," she said to Patrick, and he agreed, grumpily and gruntily, shoving his hands in his pockets: the Patrick she had known, and loved, and hated, too, since the moment he was born.

"But afterward we get to play Pinecone Bowling," he said as they started down the street. The light filtering through the trees striped his face in sun and shadow.

Liza felt she now knew many things she had not known yesterday. She knew, for example, that even rats could be beautiful, and hope grew from the smallest seeds, and sometimes there was great truth in made-up stories. She knew that the world was a complex place, and very wonderful.

Feelings, too, were complex. They could pull you in all different directions. Liza thought of the three-headed dog she had seen in the underworld, and its three snapping jaws, and the strange octopus with its razor-sharp tentacles, and how the creatures had fought to the death.

Yes, the world was very strange. But you had to walk through. That was the trick. You had to keep walking through, always, with your chin held high, the way she had passed through the shadowed tunnels of the underworld, with only the dim light of the lumpen to guide her.

That was the other trick, the other truth: Light would come to you from unexpected places.

"Someday you must remind me to tell you about the game of bowling I played Below, and how I beat the three-headed dog with the scorpion tail," Liza said as the real Patrick, her Patrick, loped beside her in the sunshine. "And I will introduce you to Mirabella. Maybe we will even go Below together—although you must absolutely promise to stay away from the River of Knowledge, and of course watch out for the scawgs. . . ."

Acknowledgments

Thank you to Maurice Sendak, and my parents for introducing me to his work;

To the continuous support of the blogger and bookseller communities;

To my agent, for his tireless campaigning on my behalf, and for being the founding member of Team Lauren Oliver;

To my editor, Rosemary Brosnan, for her attentiveness and guidance, and for whipping this book into shape;

To my sister, ever generous, wise, funny, supportive, and one of the best people on the planet;

To Lisa Zigarmi, for her unfaltering friendship, and especially for a January night several years ago;

And, lastly, to Michael Otremba. I didn't know him when I wrote this book, but since he came into my life, he has provided me with joy, inspiration, and loving support. 999,700 dates to go!